DOG FIGHT

LUCAS PEDERSON

LVP

PUBLICATIONS

Lycan Valley Press Publications
1002 N Meridian STE 100-153
Puyallup, Washington 98371
United States of America

First Edition

ISBN-13: 978-1-64562-041-9

For my son, Kollin.
Keep fighting. Keep Smiling. And never let anyone snuff out your light.
Be free.

DOG
FIGHT

CHAPTER 1

IT BURST OUT of the gate half formed and shrieking.

A single whiff of fresh piss told Lon all he needed to know about this one. A pup. Twenty or so in human years, Lon guessed. Maybe tonight was their first transformation.

Lon leaped over the shrieking creature, spun in time to dodge a partially formed claw, and lunged. The force was enough to knock the pup off balance. Lon seized the opportunity and charged. The pup was quick, though. It darted to the right, avoiding the deadly sweep of Lon's claw.

The pup's shrieks were deafening while its transformation kicked in.

Lon grunted deep in his throat and huffed through his nostrils while he circled the pup on all fours. The young creature fell onto the gravel in the throes of the change. Bones snapped and readjusted themselves. Fur sprouted, though, being a pup, the fur was patchy and sparse in most places. Especially on a misshapen face. Its eyes were wide. Its lower jaw unhinged, flapped for a second or two, revealing the pup's lashing tongue, then snapped into place… jutting outward. A shrill howl escaped its malformed muzzle.

It was now Lon became aware of the all the shouting, cheering, and booing. The cries from his master to, "Kill! KILLKILLKILLKILL! Goddamn it, NOW!" All of it struck him like a blow to the snout. During a fight, Lon had learned how to tune out the noise coming from outside the large cage. When the real fight was over all the awful noise bombarded him. A trick for old dogs.

He could kill the pup right now. It was vulnerable. Weak. There was even a part of him that wanted to. The other part, though, told him to wait. He was starving. His master trained him that way. Always be hungry, near to starving. His reward after winning a fight was to feast on his opponent. But that wasn't the only reason why he waited for the pup to change. Somewhere in the maelstrom of his mind, both man and beast, there was a smidge of rational thought. Of reason. Or maybe it was honor.

The pup would have more of a chance if it fully transformed.

Then again, maybe it was more sporting with a creature that could fight back?

Thoughts, as they were, scattered, giving him back to all the shouting and screaming and whistling. As always, their noise hurt his head and for a moment, he glanced around for a weak spot in the cage so he could shut them the fuck up.

The pup writhed on the ground, back arching, spine lengthening. Its back legs stretched, knees inverting. Bones crunched, tendons snapped. The ears grew a couple inches longer, coming to sharp, fuzzy points at the top. Its teeth disappeared into the gums only to give way for much longer, sharper fangs.

Lon continued circling the pup, heart thundering.

Soon…

Bellowing through the stew of the crowd's noise came his master's voice. Deep. Angry. Lon was failing to do what the man trained him to do. Play with the opponent enough to get the crowd riled up and make the kill as horrific as possible. The beast mind, as Lon the human thought of it as, only knew it was starving and needed to eat soon or it might get too weak. Master would put them down like he did with Max last week. Max was a good dog, too. Old, but good. Strong. Loyal. All until Max couldn't hold back the hunger anymore and was locked up for days. When it came time for his next fight, he could barely move.

Master put a bullet in his head and heart and tossed the corpse to the two pups the old man, was training.

With Max dead, Lon was now both the elder and the strongest.

Not something his human side celebrated, and the beast side didn't know why. They were the alpha now. Well, second to the Master, anyway. Not that the beast cared for whatever the human liked or didn't like. Couldn't understand much more than emotions and that was only strongest during the change.

The pup, breathing in ragged breaths, stood on its newly formed hind legs. Lon snorted while it wobbled and swayed trying to keep its balance. Not much training with this one. Very new, then. Why its master would send it in to fight didn't make any sense.

But Lon wasn't shoved, half starving, in the cage every other night to make sense of anything.

He must kill.

He must win.

There were no other options.

Kill or be killed. Eat or starve.

The outside wasn't any different by comparison. At least, as far as the bestial part of Lon remembered anyway.

The pup howled, a bit throatier this time.

Lon circled... head lowered. His upper muzzle wrinkled back in a snarl revealing sharp teeth. The pup mimicked Lon, bearing its own teeth. And, as underdeveloped they might be, would terrify any one of those shrieking things outside the cage.

The pup blinked and glanced around, as if realizing where it was for the first time. It was tossed out into a world it didn't know by its master. As if it was some kind of sacrifice.

Or ploy.

Maybe to lower Lon's guard for some surprise fight.

The beast shoved human Lon back, cutting off any trickle of thought. Thoughts the beast didn't understand fully anyway. Just a lot of noise and rambling. Alien sounds and tones. Like the crowd gathered around the dome-like cage.

The pup pounced and Lon smacked it away. It struck the ground with a yelp, rolled and sprang onto it feet for another pounce.

This time Lon leaped, met the pup in midair, and buried his teeth in its fuzzy throat. Lon slammed the creature to the ground, bit down, and ripped the pup's throat out. Blood splashed his face, momentarily blinding him. Lon grunted, swallowed the chunk of flesh and tore the pup's head off. Blood sprayed, hot and so alluring, Lon planted his mouth over the red fount and drank deeply.

The rest of the world failed to exist at that point as he plunged his claws into the pup's chest. Scarlet drool streamed from his jaws while ribs crackled, and muscles tore like wet cloth. Lon ripped out the pup's still beating heart and devoured it in a couple bites. Ragged tongue running along his muzzle, he crouched to finish the corpse off—

"Hey, dog," Master roared, cutting through the insatiable hunger. "Heel!"

Lon's jaws snapped shut. A deep growl rumbled in his throat.

No. He didn't want to stop eating. No. He didn't want to listen to Master. Every part of him tried to resist and defy Master too, but, in the end, he backed away from the delectable corpse. He kept his head low, submitting to Master. It's all in the training. Same thing he's done for as long as he could remember. Time, it seemed, really never existed for Lon. He just… was…

He didn't even remember who his mother was anymore. Nor his father. There was only Master and the other dogs in the kennel.

"I said heel," Master shouted.

Lon heard the snap before a sharp pain lashed across his back. He yelped and scrambled away from the pup's headless body.

"Back to your cage, dog!"

Lon noted the whip in Master's hands, huffed out a breath, started toward the cages, and stopped. He shot a glare at Master. Yes. He could do it right now. Kill Master. If the gate was open, maybe he could find a way to the outside before the men with guns caught him.

Master's gaze sharpened. "Back to your cage, dog." He drew a pistol from the holster on his right hip, dropping part of the whip to do so. He pointed the gun at Lon. "I said git!"

The human part of Lon's mind surfaced just enough to steer the beast away from Master back toward the cages.

The beast soon forgot the rage towards Master, which almost resulted in something bad, though hatred for the man was on the verge of boiling over.

Lon, growling, made his way through the gate and into his cage where soon the gate slid shut, locking him in.

CHAPTER 2

WHAT FELT LIKE hours crawled by.

Visitors came and went, all gawking at the prize-winning dog, Lon. Some of them spat on him. Some blew him kisses. Others tried to pet him and snapped he nipped at them. He bit off his fair share of fingers in the past of visitors who weren't quite fast enough to pull their hand out of the cage. Master hurt him if he did that, though, so he tried to let the growling and snaps be his warnings. It worked. Sometimes.

Soon enough, however, the visitors trickled away, leaving Lon alone in a gently lit room that reeked of old blood. Of rot and oil and the tang of rust. He listened to the heartbeats of the three other dogs and two pups. As slow as they were, he assumed they were sleeping. Maybe they changed back already. Odd he was the only one to fight tonight.

Other dogs from other masters howled and roared. Some whined. Other masters shouted at their dogs to, "Shut the hell up!"

Lon sighed and laid down in his cage. It was roomy enough to sprawl out. Probably the largest of all the cages. Master cared for him a little better than others, he knew that, though didn't like it. But there was nothing to be done about it.

Soon dawn would usher in morning, and then he could sleep. His human part would return, as it always did. He wondered, as much as a dog could wonder anyway, how Master treated the human part? Did that version of Lon get whipped too?

Lon closed his eyes and savored the taste of the pup's blood still on his tongue. He swallowed, drew in a breath and...

What was that?

A strange new scent snagged in his nostrils like tiny fishhooks. Lon lifted his head, straw clinging to the blood matted fur on his chin as the metal door of the room screeched open and a cage was rolled in next to his.

Now the scent was stronger. He rose onto all fours, sniffing the cage, which was draped in thick black sheets so he couldn't see in. He frowned, yet his mouth watered and... and something else in him stirred. Something he hadn't felt in a while.

Two men walked into the room, and, although he understood some of what they said and knew one was Master, his focus remained on what waited behind the black sheets of the opposite cage.

"Got two hours till dawn," a man Lon didn't know said. Sounded fat and lazy, though Lon didn't look at him. Still focused on the other cage.

"Should be enough time, I'd think," Master said. "Never let him do this before, but I think he's ready."

"Better be," the other man said. "If nothin' comes of it, consider the deal off and my payment back in full."

"Hand the fuckin' money over, Dressy," Master said. "We don't got all night. See how he's already interested?"

The two men fell quiet for a bit.

Lon stuck his snout through the bars of his cage and breathed in deep.

A female. Yes. Something about her, though. Something special…

He hadn't encountered such a scent, nor the strong stirrings in him. The *need*.

"Two hours," the man said. "Max."

"Didn't we already fuckin' agree to this?"

"Just making sure you're gonna follow through. Got you on camera too so you can't get away with shit."

Master grunted. "Think I'm a cheat, huh?"

"Never said that. I've been burned by high rollers like yourself before. Just making sure you don't fuck me over too."

"Two hours," Master said. "Give me her key and get the fuck out."

Lon spared a glance at Master, watched the other man step out of the room, and returned his attention to the female behind the black sheets. She smells so beautiful. Delicious, even. He wants to know her. He's never had a companion, except for

Max. And even then, Max was more like a father figure. Was she like him? He couldn't quite tell through the thick sheets.

Master cleared his throat, getting Lon's attention.

"Be gentle, Ol'Hoss," Master said. "First time for both of ya." He grunted and patted the female's cage. A soft whine filtered through the sheets and a pang of anger struck Lon. He didn't know why, but right then, he wanted to rip Master's head off and bash his skull into the floor until brains splattered.

"You're a winner." Master winked at Lon. "You'll be gettin' a lot of bitches now. Might turn ya into a breedin' stud soon. Easy street if ya can pull it off."

Lon had no idea what Master was talking about and didn't care. What mattered was the female in the cage next to his. Yes. She smelled so… delicious. Not food-wise, but something else.

"Okay," Master said and turned to the female's cage. "Ya got two hours, big fella." He unlocked both cages and walked to the doorway. "Make it count. Lot of money ridin' on this deal." He closed the door and locked it.

Lon glanced at the female's cage. There were no sounds. He looked at the door of his cage and nudged it open. The hinges gave shrill cries like terrified children. He slipped out of the cage and moved toward the female, head lowered, gaze fixed on the black flap of sheet covering her door.

He stopped and backed away. Maybe she was too scared? He crouched near the center of the room, directly under the light, and gave a light whine. Maybe if he showed her that he meant no harm, maybe…

After some time and few more whines, her cage door slowly opened, taking the black sheet with it.

Lon blinked, heart stuttering as a pair of silvery eyes caught the light a second before his own eyes adjusted to the darkness of her cage. His breath caught in his throat. Yes. She was beautiful. And with the sheet moved, he inhaled her full aroma. A shiver trembled along his spine and all the strength trickled out of him for a moment or two.

She stepped out of the cage on all fours, head lowered, green eyes fixed on him. Her white fur appeared to glow under the gentle light. A thing so radiant compared to the gloom of the room. She paused, cocked her head to the side.

Lon rose on all fours and slowly approached her. A thin whine gathered in his throat. He wanted to know her. Feel her next to him while they slept. Her warmth. The comfort.

That's all he wanted, until she turned and walked toward the other side of the room. Another scent struck him hard across the snout, obliterating the want of comfort and warmth and replacing it with an undeniable *need*. Something he felt before but had been so long ago it might as well be a brand-new sensation. His groin stirred. Saliva filled his mouth and drooled onto the floor. His heart hammered. Faster. Faster.

The female glanced back at him once she reached the other side of the room and that's all it took.

He pounced on her, claws digging deep into her back. She yelped but didn't try to move away or fight him. She moaned when he plunged his sex into her over and over. She cried out when his grip tightened, claws digging deeper into her flesh, and he shot his seed into her. Blood dripped onto the floor from the wounds. Still, she did not try to fight him or get away. Instead, she arched and pressed herself into him. And when he was finished, carefully pulling his claws and sex out of her, she turned around and nuzzled into his broad chest.

Exquisitely exhausted, Lon and the female laid down in front of their cages, snuggled close to each other, limbs entwined.

He breathed in her delicious scent, sighed and lowered his head. He soon drifted into a deep sleep, happy for what felt like the first time in forever.

CHAPTER 3

"GIT!"

Something smacked his ribs hard enough for the pain to yank him out of sleep.

"I said, git, ya fuckin' dog!"

Lon sucked in his sharp breath went to sit up but soon realized he was snuggled up to someone. He blinked away the blurriness of sleep and could only stare. Even while the man continued yelling at him to, "Git".

A woman snoozed on his left arm; face buried mostly in his chest. But who—

"Git'way from m'bitch, dog!"

Another heavy smack to the ribs. Another shot of pain.

Lon glanced around but didn't recognize the room. Where did the old man take them now? And who was the bastard yelling at him?

"Hey." Lon recognized the grizzled voice of the old man. Somewhere between an older Burgess Meredith and Tom Waits, maybe. Only a little deeper and scarier sounding. "Hit my dog one more time and I'll blow your fuckin' head off."

"Been four hours," the other man said. "Deal was for two."

"Looks like the deed was done, though, eh?"

"How the fuck should I know?"

A heavy sigh. "Take your bitch and get lost. I'll have my people keep an eye on ya."

Lon rose, carefully moving the woman aside so her head didn't hit the cement floor, and towered face to face with a scrawny man with long greasy hair and a white scar running diagonally across his leathery face. His bright blue eyes squinted at Lon.

"Whatcha want, dog? Best git in yer cage 'fore I kick ya in there m'self."

"You ain't gonna be kickin' shit," the old man said and lifted the woman from the floor.

She gasped, eyes wide, trying to figure out where she was and what happened. Lon knew the feeling. It was becoming daily routine to wake up somewhere new with strangers gawking at him. Her gaze stuck on Lon for a long time before the old man shoved her into scar-face's arms.

"Said take your bitch and leave," the old man said. "Didn't I? Keep it up and the deal is off and I get the pup."

Scar-face glowered at the old man for a moment, grunted, and hauled the woman away.

Lon started to follow. The woman might be in danger. She—

"Another step and ya get the whip, Lon.'

Lon stopped. He knew what the whip was, just like he knew he turned into a monster every night. Just like he knew the old man made the creature part of him fight other creatures for money. But what was the woman for? His mind was too foggy to latch onto anything. He needed coffee. Food. A shower.

Once scar-face and the woman were gone, the old man tapped Lon on the shoulder. Lon turned and to his surprise, the old man was smiling. Something so rare, Lon blinked several times to make sure he wasn't hallucinating.

"That bitch is gonna make us rich, boyo."

Lon frowned, cleared his throat and managed a whispery, "What?"

A couple men Lon didn't recognize came in and set up two chairs and card table. Two other men followed behind with silver platters heaping with steamy food and a pitcher of what could be coffee or water.

They set the table and left the room without a word.

The old man gestured at the table. "How 'bout we get somethin' to eat? I'm starvin'."

Lon glanced down at his nakedness and back at the old man. The old man chuckled.

"Oh, yeah." From a small leather satchel, he brought out a pair of black sweatpants and black t-shirt. "Here ya go."

Lon got dressed and met the old man at the table, who was already seated and pouring himself a cup of coffee. So, it was coffee then. The aroma food and coffee… Lon kept swallowing so he wouldn't drool all over himself.

"Sit, Lon," the old man said.

Lon sat in the chair across from the old man. He watched this man who stole everything from him years ago, shovel forkfuls of scrambled eggs into his mouth and hated him even more. The bastard did like his eggs. Also liked to mess with Lon. If Lon tried to eat his food the old man might shock him with an electric cow prod, something. Part of the training, the old man would always quip.

No. Lon sat and watched the old man eat, stomach groaning in hunger. He didn't dare pick up a fork or look at his plate.

And yet, the old man frowned, swallowed and gestured to the food. "Eat, Lon. It's okay. No training today."

Lon blinked. Could it be a trick? Another form of training, perhaps? Lon picked the fork up beside his plate and stabbed a clump of scrambled eggs. He paused, glanced at the old man.

"Oh, for Christ sake, boy." The old man waved a meaty hand at Lon's plate. "I swear to ya. No trainin' right now. Chow down!"

Lon brought the forkful of egg to his mouth and eat it. He swallowed quickly and shot a glance at the old man once more. But the guy was too busy devouring his own plate of food to notice this time so Lon, throwing caution to the wind for the first time since he could remember, ate a real breakfast. Eggs. Bacon. Sausages. Pancakes. And coffee.

He finished his plate before the old man. Never since the old man had he eaten so well. There were faint memories of his mother. Sunday mornings with a plate pull of food and a tall glass of orange juice. Of his mom humming away to some tune on the radio in the kitchen while she finished cooking the last of the pancakes. The warm morning sun filtered through the small dining room windows which kissed the tips of his ears and embraced the back of his head. His little sister, Emmy, telling him they should climb that tree in the back yard Mom said was too dangerous around a mouthful of pancakes. Syrup dribbling down her chin.

The memories of his old life flooded back like that sometimes. All at once. When everything seemed so simple and he didn't turn into a monster every goddamn night. Before his mom died...

"Good, eh?" The old man said and took a deep swig from his coffee cup.

Lon nodded, sipping his own coffee; trying to savor it. He was still waiting for the old man to flip the table and whip him or tase him or some kind of punishment for "falling for kindness", or something as asinine.

When the old man belched and leaned back in the folding chair, his considerable weight forcing a few creaks and groans from it, Lon knew he would be okay. The old man was content. Not a glint of mean in his beady, dark eyes. Only an unusual gleam Lon only saw when money was being offered.

"Yes," the old man said. "Good stuff." He patted his belly and smiled at Lon. "Today might be the beginning of an easier life, Lonny, m'boy."

Lon lowered his cup of coffee. "What do you mean?"

The old man snorted. "You're getting' old, Lon. Forty is over prime for fightin'."

Lon frowned, took another sip of coffee.

"Ha." The old man leaned forward and slapped a hand on the table. The coffee pitcher clinked against Lon's silver plate. "If that bitch gets pregnant, boyo, all you're gonna be fightin' are the other bitches tryin' to get your jizz."

Realization finally struck Lon like a hard slap across the face. "You made him mate?"

The old man tossed back his head and barked laughter at the ceiling.

When the laughter subsided, the man pointed at Lon. "*You* did the deed, Lon! Don't go blamin' the creature. You both had a hand in it, even if you didn't know."

Hatred for the old man swelled. "W-Why?"

"Oh, come on now, Lon." The old man stood and paced the room a bit. "Thought this would be good for us. Both gettin' older. Gotta think about retirement, ya know? No more fightin'. Just fuckin'. Well, for you anyway." He giggled and Lon instantly hated the sound. "You're the top dog, boyo. Number one! The breeders are callin' and wantin' your seed now. Give'em pups from good stock, ya know."

Lon placed his coffee cup on the table. "Good stock."

"Yes," the old man said, hell, nearly shouted. He stopped pacing and pointed at Lon. "You know how much money this will make me? Enough to buy both my kids houses and vehicles." His gaze drifted away from Lon. "We could move to somewhere nice. Like Hawaii or somewhere in the Caribbean. Our own goddamn island!" There was no denying the man was in a state of ecstasy now. "Easy street, boyo. Jus think of it. All the honeys and sun you want. Not a care in the world…"

Lon, still frowning at the old man, refilled his coffee cup and drank. He didn't respond to the old man because it didn't matter if he did or not. The decision had been made.

Still, the coffee woke him up. Got his brain working and his heart rate up. Thoughts unfurled from their dormant cocoons. How long had it been since he drank coffee? Years? He couldn't remember but years felt about right. The old man might as well be his father. The one who abandoned his mom when Lon and his sister were only about six or seven years old. Just up and gone and never heard from again.

The old man sat down, poured himself more coffee and drank. He pointed at Lon. "Drink up. We're not done with the fights yet. Couple more months to see if the bitch is pregnant. After that, we'll start planning for the future." He winked. "Ya think you got another couple fights left in ya, boyo?"

He hated that nickname. Boyo. What the fuck did that even mean? Boyo…

Lon's glare rose from the cup to the old man.

The old man smiled. "Oh, yes. Ya got a good couple fights in ya for sure. Can see it in those eyes." He leaned back a bit. "That's why I picked you out of the litter, ya know?"

Lon blinked. "Litter?" He didn't remember anything about a litter.

"Well, yeah. How old were ya back then? Shit, I can't remember. Sixteen? Seventeen?" He snapped his fingers, eyes widening. "That's it. Seventeen. Rogue dog broke in an' killed your fam…" The old man stopped himself and looked away. All of a sudden, he appeared embarrassed or lost. "Well, someone found ya and put you in with a few other pups. I saw the fight in your eyes." He downed the rest of his coffee and stood. "Okay. Get some shuteye, boyo. We're gonna be rich."

The old man started off toward the doorway.

"What do you mean a rogue dog broke in?" Lon stood. "Is that why I'm like this? Because I survived a dog attack?"

The old man's shoulders slumped. A heavy sigh rose into the air. And when he turned around, Lon noticed he appeared worried. Scared…

"Took a lot of training for you to forget what happened, Lon. I really don't want to undo all that work right now. Let's get through these next couple fights and I'll tell ya everything you want to know." He smiled a bit. "Sound good?"

If Lon had been stuck in the usual weary state after a change, maybe he would have agreed, but today the coffee awakened something in him. A fire he thought was forever lost for him and only given to the creature within.

"No."

The old man's smile fell away. His bushy gray eyebrows knitted together in a deep frown. "The hell ya mean, 'no'?"

Lon moved closer to the old man. "I want to know now."

"The fuck has gotten into you, Lon?" The old man began backing away towards the door. "I said we'll talk about it after the last couple fights."

"I know," Lon said, moving even closer. "But I want to know now."

All the fear was instantly replaced with hate. Hate for this old man who kept him kenneled for so long for no other reason but to make money.

"Look," the old man said, reaching for his whip, which wasn't on his hip at the moment. He sighed, though didn't stop his slow progress backward. "I saved you. I—"

"You made me a *slave*." Lon rushed forward, grabbed the old man by the collar of his shirt, yanked him back and glared into his wide eyes. "You made me entertain rich people to line your own pockets while starving me and the others nearly to death."

The old man yanked out of Lon's grip, tearing his shirt in the process. "And look where you are now, ya ungrateful cur." Breathing heavily, he pointed at Lon. "You'd be dead right now if I hadn't picked you from that litter."

"Fuck you."

The old man gasped. It was the first time Lon had ever really stood up for himself. First time having coffee in many years too. Combined it created an explosion too massive to control.

"Wh-What did you just say to me?" The old man backed away. He collided with the table of empty plates and a partial pot of coffee. Everything crashed and clattered to the floor.

Lon watched the last of the coffee glug from the

broken top of the pot then focused his attention on the old man.

"Goddamn it, Lon," the old man said, somehow keeping his balance and trundling through the mess on the floor. "You know better. Git to your cage!"

And, for a second or two, he stopped. His gaze floated to the large cage in the corner. A part of him wanted to obey because part of him knew that without the old man, he probably would be dead. The old man was right about that.

But... what if death was better than a life of slavery. First in fighting, then in breeding more monsters like himself.

Being whipped for the first time by the old man. It recycled through his caffeinated mind now. Over and over and—

The old man held a butter knife in his trembling right hand. He brandished it at Lon. "The fuck you gonna do, dog? Huh? I own you! I've always owned you! Now git in your goddamn cage!"

"Money," Lon said, moving closer. "That's all you care about. It was never about saving our lives."

The old man opened his mouth. His lower jaw jittered a bit before his mouth shut again. The old man glowered at Lon and took him at least a minute to respond. "Did what I had to. Dog fights were a growing trend and when I saw you and Max, I figured why not?"

"So, instead of raising and loving us, you chose to profit from us," Lon said, voice turning to a hiss on the last word.

The old man slashed the butter knife at Lon. "I saved you! Might not be the life ya wanted, but it's what ya got. Stop this bullshit right now or I'll—"

"Slap me to death with your butter knife?" Lon chuckled and closed the gap between them. He slammed the old man against the wall, hand clutching the flabby throat. The old man released a strangled sound and tried to stab Lon with the butter knife.

Lon yanked the butter knife out of the old man's hand and tapped it against the man's wrinkly forehead. "Tell me what happened to my family."

The old man tried prying himself from the grip on his throat and Lon kneed him in the gut. The old man squealed and dropped to his knees clutching his belly. His mouth opened and closed like a dying fish. A tiny sound Lon couldn't describe floated from the open mouth.

Lon rolled his eyes and lifted the old man back onto his feet and pulled him close. "If you don't tell me, I'll cut your throat out." He held the butterknife between them. The silver glimmered in the old man's wide, terrified eyes.

It took a second or three for the old man to catch his breath. When he did, he said, "I... fuck... I did what I had to do, okay?" He coughed, spraying Lon's face with spittle.

Lon slid the dull blade of the butterknife along one of the old man's bushy, gray eyebrows and grinned. "Did you?"

"Yes," the old man cried. "You're alive aren't you?"

Lon snorted. "Alive?" He slipped the blade of the butterknife under the old man's right eyeball. The old man shrieked, clawing at Lon's arm, kicking with his stubby legs. Lon slammed him harder into the concrete wall. "I've been your *slave* for years. Not alive…"

Lon pushed down on the handle of the butterknife.

The old man screamed. His struggles deteriorated into submission, and he dropped to his knees again, body quaking. The eyeball didn't quite pop out like Lon thought it would. Rather, it bulged out of the socket, on the verge of popping out and dangling on the old man's pale cheek.

Sobbing, the old man reached for Lon. He slapped the trembling hands away.

"What happened to my family?" Lon said, much louder now. Almost a shout. He didn't want to get too loud and draw attention to the room. The old man had a few handlers he employed. They would be coming around soon too.

The old man's good eye blinked. He tried pushing his bulging eyeball back, though to no avail. After a few attempts, he lowered his head and sobbed.

"Tell me," Lon said.

"What's there to fuckin' tell, you fuckin' cur," the old man spat. "A dog killed them. Tore your mom to ribbons and tossed her remains all over the living room. Your sister's head was found in the toilet bowl. That what you want to know? Huh?" The old man looked at Lon, a runner of saliva trickled down the side of his whiskery chin. "Wanna hear how many times the coroner said your mom was raped too?"

Lon lowered the butter knife, heart stuttering. He

shook his head and stumbled away from the old man.

"Didn't fuckin' think so," the old man said and tried once more to put his eye back in. Again, to no avail. He sighed, fighting away sobs. "Now git your ass in that cage and make us millionaires!"

Lon's legs were like stacks of pencil erasers. He swayed and wobbled backward, still shaking his head.

Eventually, he said, "And it bit me?"

"No, it pissed on you." The old man placed a hand over his bulging eye while the other glowered at Lon. "Of course, it fuckin' bit you! You sure as hell weren't born a dog. We would've already been rich by now."

Lon didn't know what to expect but a dog, like himself, tearing his family apart wasn't it. Had he assumed he'd been bitten? Yes. But all these years in a stupor while in his human form and the old man's training and... just everything. He never fully let his mind wrap around the issue. Coffee woke him up. Literally.

And yet, he still wasn't sure he could belicve the old man. It could all be just a ploy to get him to give up and go back to his cage. A way of control... of slavery...

"Git back in your cage!"

Lon straightened and glared at the old man. "No."

The old man's good eye blinked. "What?" He shuffled closer to Lon. "What did you just say to me?"

"I said, no." Lon stood inside the doorway now.

"It might be days before they find you in here."

The old man froze. "What are you talking about?"

Lon backed into the hall beyond the door to the room. "There's a water bowl in the cage." He slammed the metal door shut and ran all three heavy sliding bolts home. Top. Middle. Bottom. At least four inches thick each. Barely audible, the old man wailed.

He stared at the door from a side he had never seen before. The outside.

Free, he thought. *Fr—*

A thin whine floated through the air, drawing his attention to the left. About ten feet from his door, he found another door. Same as his... metal with thick steel sliding bolts. He frowned, listening. But the whining sound didn't come again.

He backed away, was about to make a run for it, when someone from the other side of the door said, "Save me. Please. I know you're out there."

Lon glanced back and forth, heart thrumming. The old man's guards could appear at any moment.

"P-Please. Help me."

It sounded like a child. Could be one of the pups.

He spared another glance up and down the hall and pulled all three sliding bolts back. Each gave a shrill shriek that echoed throughout the hall.

"It's unlocked," Lon said and walked away.

He was no more than twenty feet down the hall, passing by yet another metal door, when the squeal of metal-on-metal hinges assaulted his hearing. He stopped and glanced over his shoulder. A lanky figure draped in shadows slinked into the hall. A long sigh followed.

Lon nodded and started walking again.

A giggle bounced off the concrete walls.

Lon stopped walking. This time he turned around, a frown washing over his face. At first, he didn't see the thing. Then it moved and the light from one of the fluorescents caught its eyes. Narrow, silvery eyes.

Another giggle shivered the air.

"You okay?" Lon said, frown deepening. He started to back away a bit.

"Why... yesss... I'm free, ain't I?" The creature giggled. Not high pitched, nor low, but somewhere in the middle. Just enough to grate on Lon's nerves. Like nails slowly dragging across a blackboard. Annoying, yet a little terrifying.

"You are," Lon said. "Look, we need to move. The guards will be—"

"Hungry," it said and shifted out of the shadows into the light.

Lon blinked. His heart stuttered. It crawled on all fours, mostly transformed, yet... there was something wrong. Skin so pale it was nearly translucent. No fur covered the lanky body. Its elongated arms were roped with muscle, its claws unnaturally long. Its sharp nails clicked on the tiled floor. A grin spread along its misshapen head. Something close to canine yet stopped short with barely a snout. Long, pointy teeth glinted under the lights. A runner of silvery drool clung from its whiskery, white chin.

"What the fuck happened to you?" It was all Lon

could think of to say.

"Hungry…" the creature said and lowered its malformed head.

Lon's mind shuffled through different responses and only landed on one. "You want Master?"

The creature paused and cocked its head. The runner of drool gooped to the floor.

"He's in that room over there." Lon pointed at the room only a couple feet diagonal from the creature.

It turned a bit, looked at the door and snorted, taking in whatever scents it could with that smooshed snout. It reminded Lon of the pug their neighbor lady owned when he was a kid. Nice lady. Lovely dog, though not like the dog Lon would eventually become.

Nor like the creature snorting around the bottom of the metal door to Lon's room.

"Just pull the bolts," Lon said. "He's all yours."

It snorted, glanced at Lon, then returned its attention to the metal door. A guttural growl issued from the abomination. Lon didn't know what happened to it. Was there a strange disease going around with his kind now? If so, the old man never mentioned it, nor took any precautions.

Lon backed away while the creature pulled the first bolt.

Reeeee…

The creature grasped the second bolt and Lon backed away some more. The thing appeared to not even acknowledge him anymore. Still, he back stepped, keeping his gaze on the creature. His pace was moderate so not to trigger the monster's attack response.

Reeee, went the second bolt.

From within the room, the old man was calling out for help.

The creature giggled, and it wasn't even a human giggle. Sounded more like a hyena. Lon, still keeping an eye on the creature, backed down the hall until he came to a corner and slowly slipped around it. He sighed, turned and hurried away.

He wasn't far when the old man began to scream.

CHAPTER 4

THEY MUST NOT have heard the old man's scream or were checking in on the other dogs, because Lon hurried from hall to hall without encountering a single guard.

Soon enough, he found what he hoped he wouldn't find. A gate made of thick bars. At least four inches thick. Locked.

"Shit," he said and slammed a fist against bars.

He spun around, looking for another way out. There had to be another way, right? A hall stretched out before him, though appeared unlit after about twenty or thirty yards down. He glanced over his shoulder at the locked gate, heart thrumming, then back down the darkened hall. He armed sweat from his forehead, sighed, and started down the hall.

The walls began to change the farther he ventured. From concrete to stone. And once he stepped out of the light, a strange smell wisped through the air. Something earthy. Like dirt and wet dead leaves on a chilly, rainy, October night. He couldn't see anything so held his arms out in front of him like a blind man. He swept them slowly back and forth.

A soft plinking sound, like dripping water found his hearing.

Something behind him moved. A foot or shoe slipping along the concrete floor. Quick. Stealthy.

Lon's heart hammered. He swallowed down a growing lump in his throat. A shiver trickled along his spine.

He was about to give up when dim light appeared ahead. Little more than a pinprick in the darkness. The shuffling sound behind him stopped. He wondered if it was the other dog? Was it stalking him now? The thought sent a fresh series of shivers through him. There was no use turning around. Not as dark as it was in the hall. If it wanted to kill him now, it could do so without much effort.

But as the pinprick grew larger and larger becoming a reinforced window in a metal door it became apparent nothing was behind him. Just to be sure, he turned around and listened. His gaze scanned over the darkness just beyond the pale touch of light filtering through the grimy window. No sounds except for water dripping. The shadows did not stir.

Lon returned his attention to the door and tried the latch, knowing it wouldn't open. Already knowing it was locked…

The latch squealed when he pushed down, and

the door clicked open.

The old man must have forgotten to lock it, assuming this was the way he entered.

Could also be a trap. Maybe the guard already knew about his escape. Maybe they were waiting for him on the other side of the door? Ready to gun him down and decapitate him. What were the other things one was supposed to do to make sure a dog remained dead? Stuff the heart with wolfsbane and burn it?

Something like that, but he couldn't remember. He couldn't even remember if his dog side killed its opponents or mutilated them enough for the guards or whoever to perform a real death. Lon wasn't too sure about the whole wolfsbane thing, though. Sounded more like some godawful fairy tale joke. About as stupid as silver bullets.

Lon opened the door. It groaned, but not very loud. He stepped through and closed the door and froze when it made a loud metallic clank. He stood there, sweat trickling down his face, heart bashing against his ribs, breath held, for what felt like hours.

When nothing happened, Lon took in his surroundings. A concrete stairwell stood not far in front of him. On either side he was blocked by walls made of large limestone slabs stacked and mudded to perfection. Indeed, no stone appeared out of place. Even the ragged edges appeared to align.

Lon drew in a breath, blew it out, and ventured up the stairs.

A couple flights or so and he came to another door. Metal, like all the others. This one, however, didn't have a normal latch or knob. Instead, it boasted a push door latch. Like in school or a hospital. Just needed to push the latch to open it.

Again, he figured it'd be locked, but, again, he pushed the door open without any issues.

This time, however, he waited longer, keeping the door partially open for at least five minutes. He kept his senses sharp, but the only sounds were the birds in the trees and a breeze flowing through the bushes near the door. There was a mixture of smells, but not being in his dog form, could only catch whiffs of gasoline, freshly cut grass, and something else he couldn't place. Rotten bananas?

Yes. Something like that. Rotting fruit. Sweet decay…

Lon opened the door and stepped outside. The door clicked behind him. He stood in a shallow alcove of a low-lying building. It wasn't the usual room Lon had woken up in, so he wasn't sure if it was the building the old man raised him in. His veritable home.

Squinting a bit from the harsh sunlight, he drew in a breath of the outside world. Something he had tasted over the years and knew once before the old man, but always tried to savor. The taste of freedom. The air was free. Something he longed to be. Free.

Still, it took him a long time to move away from the door and onto a gravel walkway. He glanced around and all he could see were trees full of green, a building covered in thick moss, and the gravel walkway. He closed his eyes and just breathed. He listened to the birds. Somewhere nearby, something scampered through the woods. A squirrel?

Chipmunk? Weasel? The gentle caress of a warm breeze around his sweaty, naked body told him it was summer.

Naked...

For the first time in a long time, Long glanced down at himself and realized he wasn't wearing any pants. Not even underwear. Or socks. Nothing. He stood outside the only home he had ever know, and not ever really known for that matter, completely nude.

Still, there was a tiny bit of embarrassment that crept in. Even if he had been naked after a lot of the dog fights it never much registered and right now, it did, for some damn reason.

Maybe it was a callback from his earlier life. A life of luxury, even if they were struggling. It was better than being a dog under the old man's "care", anyway. Still, he wore actual clothes. No matter how poor they were. Mom always took care of him and his sister.

His sister...

What was her name?

He couldn't remember.

So long ago when the dog the old man told him about tore them apart. There were bits and pieces. Sparks in the dark.

Lon shook his head and glanced around. The gravel walkway was clear, and he didn't hear anyone approaching. No scuffing boots through the small rocks. He stood at a T intersection from the door. But which way led to freedom? Which way could he escape unnoticed?

He went right, and it didn't take him long to

come across a small station placed out in the woods with one guard inside and three others standing outside. Somehow, they didn't see him, and he backed away to the T intersection.

He went left, and encountered another station like the right and returned to the T.

Lon glanced back and forth, heart thundering. He didn't want to go back. He *couldn't* go back.

Left… or right… ?

His stomach churned. The birds sang sweet praises. Squirrels scampered and the sun baked onto the top of his head. He was about to say fuck it and return to his room and forget everything when something moved in front of him. Lon blinked, frowned, and glanced at the movement.

It took a few seconds to notice the small rabbit hopping in the woods in front of him while it snacked on clovers and flowers and raspberries. Lon squinted, then his gaze lifted, piercing into the woods. He didn't see a station out there among the trees and all the green. There could be, but so far… he didn't see it.

"Fuck it," he whispered and hurried into the woods.

Sticks snapped under his bare feet. Thorny brambles snagged and cut his legs up to the thighs. Bugs lit on his sweat sheened skin and feasted on him. Mosquitos and gnats. Flies. Strange beetles he couldn't name. But he refused to stop or slow down. No matter how much he hurt or itched. The need to get as far away from the place the old man kept him in for so long, his prison, tossed everything else to the wayside.

Freedom.

Yes.

Freedom was through the woods. Through the thorns and sticks and rocks and bugs. He pushed onward. No matter how much his feet bled, or how nature tried to shred the skin from his naked body, Lon pushed onward. At one point, while crawling up a steep hill, sweat cascading down his face, dark hair in wet, clotted strings over his eyes, he thought he heard something howl behind him.

He stopped a several times, waiting for any sign someone or something might be following him, but it was all wasted time. Light leaked from the day. He didn't know what time it was when he left his slave quarters, nor was he sure of how long he'd been running through the woods. Hell, he didn't even know if he was in the United States or not.

The fighting circuit was huge, he knew, but just *how* huge? Worldwide?

Lon, gasping, dropped to his knees in a hollow filled with lily of the valleys. The air was getting hotter and humid. Coupled with all the vegetation and the aroma of the flowers, it was like a thick, noxious green soup. He coughed and sat in a pond of fragrant white trying to breathe. His heart might as well be a rubber ball bouncing off the walls of his chest.

Gradually, he caught his breath and began breathing regularly. Didn't change the fact that the air was still humid as Hell's asshole.

He tried to stand, but his legs failed him. His body trembled.

Pushed too hard, Lon thought. He sighed and

glanced around at all the white blooms. Except for a couple of fallen trees, the flowers had taken over the small patch of land. Once he got used to the smell it didn't bother him much, even with the humidity.

Still, he couldn't stand and no matter how much time he waited... his body refused.

Years of being cooped up in that place. Of the same routine over and over and over. The training. The days and nights. Of barely being aware if he had to piss or not.

It wasn't just the coffee that woke him up, he realized while lying down in the pond of flowing white, the old man forgot to drug him. Or maybe it was intentional?

He didn't know how far away he was from the underground building he lived in for so many years and didn't care. The familiar weariness wrapped him in white gauze. As white as the flowers surrounding him in this quaint hollow in the woods. Somewhere nearby, a crow cawed.

The world around him dimmed. The sounds turned to wavy, sardonic echoes. Like someone singing through a long PVC pipe.

Lon drew a breath of sweet lilies... and the gray fog swept over him.

CHAPTER 5

AN ORCHESTRA OF crickets and frogs obscured his hearing followed by a strange, sweet scent clouding his nostrils.

Lon sneezed and scrambled to all fours, a deep growl rumbling his throat. He darted back and forth through flowers, gaze shifting, nostrils flaring. He didn't know where he was. Not in the cage or even a room. Where was Master? He crawled out of a hollow filled with strange flowers he couldn't name and stood on his hind legs to get away from the overpowering stench of the flowers.

A slight breeze ruffled the fur around his neck, and he shivered. His green eyes blinked at all the trees and foliage. At the raccoon perched in a branch not far above his head. At the crickets that scurry and chirp. At the owl hooting not far from where he stood.

Something inside him shuddered. His eyes widened.

Free.

He was finally free.

And he thought he'd been dreaming his human part escaping Master's house…

No. It hadn't been a dream.

He was free.

Really free.

Lon inhaled, drawing in all the scents he could. He moved around the hollow of flowers and ventured deeper into the woods.

It was almost like being born again. Everything… so new. So different. He glanced at the night sky while the tree canopy swayed in another breeze, shifting just enough for him to see the dusting of sparkling stars. He marveled over the sight until the breeze ebbed and the canopy closed. He drew in a long, deep breath, tasting new scents on his tongue as well as smelling them. Some new, others not, but everything was so fresh. Clean. No dank basement mold or stench of shit and piss from the other dogs and himself.

Lon released his held breath, having savored the freshness enough, and glanced around once more.

He was in the woods, but why?

Brief echoes of what happened with his human part blipped through his already overwhelmed mind. He caught a glimpse of Master's shocked face and then some kind of creature stepping out of the shadows. Another dog? If so, this one appeared to be sick.

The images shuffled through and disappeared,

leaving him to gape into the night woods... lost.

Free...

His heart galloped at the very thought. Free. No more fights. No more people. Just... just the woods and him. He howled at the night, the happiest he's been since he could remember. Free. Now he could roam. Now he could *live*. Now...

A strange, yet delicious scent hooked his nostrils. He turned, tasting the air for a minute or two before finally pinpointing a direction. Saliva, hot and suffocating filled his mouth. He gulped it down and shot forward through the woods. No idea where he was going or what his senses screamed at him to eat. Just... go. Just devour.

Eat...

Hunger ravaged his insides. Master wouldn't let him eat until he killed something in the cage with all those people watching. But now... now he was free. Now, why... he could eat anything he wanted and not stop until he had his fill. No one to tell him no. No one starve him. No one to make him fight for his life. No more whips.

Free...

Lon grinned and shot into the woods. He sprinted through the cool air, nose to the wind. Various scents and foliage caressed his passing. He dodged various trees and leapt over thick brambles filled with sharp thorns. Something. A small animal. Raccoon? Started up a tree and Lon pounced, catching the critter with his teeth and ripping it from the tree. Blood, hot and delicious filled his mouth. He slammed the animal to the ground and tore into it. Most of the raccoon was gone by the time he caught another scent. This one was musky, though not very noticeable.

He grunted and ran toward the musky aroma on all fours. Something new. Never in his life had he smelled something both so alluring and compelling. Didn't matter, though, he wanted to find out what tripped all the instinctive triggers. He soon slid to a stop, momentarily losing the creature's scent. He crouched low, hiding in a thick patch of tall grass. The breeze had shifted a bit, causing the lapse in scent. Above, the canopy whispered like conspiring voices. The trees swayed ever so slightly, groaning.

Except for those sounds, the woods fell silent. Not even the crickets chirped.

Something was in the woods.

Something nature knew didn't belong.

Lon, heart thrumming, waited as long as he could. He slipped quietly out of the grass, turning different directions. Standing and crouching. But whatever he smelled before was gone. Or it found a way to mask its scent.

Gradually, the night came back to life around him. The crickets and frogs continued their nightly orchestra, the bats squeaked, and the owls hooted their displeasure of it all.

Another scent drew his mind away from the strange one he lost. This scent was light. Almost oily. Slippery. He didn't know what it was but knew he needed to check it out. So, he sprinted toward the oily scent until, almost, running directly into it.

Maybe it was hunting him too.

He jumped off a nearby tree, landed and it immediately spotted the large cat. His human part said it was a mountain lion. It screeched at him, followed by a deep growl in its throat. It lowered its head a bit, nostrils working. It was trying to identify Lon, but judging by its hesitation it couldn't.

Lon darted forward. The cat hissed and swept its paws in the air while backing up. Lon stopped. He growled and relished in the other predator's eyes widening a bit. It glanced down, away, then back at Lon. In his experience fighting, Lon came to know the signs of submission. The mountain lion knew it wasn't a match for Lon, so it was looking for a way out of the situation.

With a grunt, Lon sprang forward and tore the cat's head from its body. Blood sprayed and Lon clamped his mouth over the hot fount, drinking deeply. Eventually the spray eased. He slurped down a few more mouthfuls of blood and chomped a chunk out of the stump of neck.

When Lon had his fill of the large cat, hunger satisfied for now, he wandered through the woods. He had no destination and really just wanted to find a place to sleep. Maybe this was why Master starved him? Still, he relished the sensation of being full. All kinds of sounds bombarded him from every direction, but he found they didn't matter.

He stumbled into a thicket, scaring up a doe and her fawn, and collapsed. His stomach churned and he had a second or two to wonder if he might have eaten too much when he jetted vomit onto a bed of tamped down grass, dead leaves, and deer fur. He crawled deeper into the thicket, vomited again... then knew no more.

CHAPTER 6

IT WAS THE birds that woke him with their constant and infuriating songs.

But the buzzing kept him awake.

Lon rolled onto his back and squinted at the sun filtering through the canopy. He groaned and rolled onto his side where he came face to face with something rancid. He opened his eyes a bit more and scooted away from a large pile of twisted hide and chewed gore. Flies trundled over the mess.

Something cold pressed against his back. The buzzing increased for a few seconds, ebbed, then returned to the same, irritating noise. And when he glanced over his shoulder he gagged at another pile of gore, though smaller than the last.

Lon, gagging, crawled out of a thicket and into the damp leaves and weeds of a late morning. Or at least he assumed so, with the position of the sun nearing its height to full noon in the sky. Wait, was that even right? He read it somewhere but didn't know for sure. Maybe it didn't matter. All he knew was it felt like morning. Cool and everything still beaded with dew.

The smell was getting to him. The stench of rotting meat.

His other half must have fed well last night. Too well. It left mutilated corpses only partially eaten. What they were before it got to them, Lon couldn't even guess. Animals from the forest. Maybe a deer and raccoon?

Lon stood, covering his private area with trembling hands and glanced around for a shelter or something to help cover himself up, at least. But the world around him was all green and trees. No signs of civilization. Not even a hunting shack. Just… green. And trees. And bugs.

He wouldn't be able to live out here for long. He didn't know any survival skills or how to really build a shelter. He needed to find a town. A place to hole up for a bit. Find clothes and figure out what the hell he was going to do now. He didn't have an identity, that much he knew from the Old Man telling him over and over throughout training. He was nothing. A ghost. No records of him existed anywhere, according to the Old Man.

Shivering, he made his way through the woods. His throat ached for water, but he didn't trust any of the tiny streams he stepped over. He read somewhere a person could get sick by drinking water from creeks like that. So… he plodded onward, naked and welcoming the summer heat when it finally penetrated the forest canopy.

Sometime in the afternoon, his stomach made a thick groaning sound. Pain slithered through his lower abdomen. Heat built in his bowels.

Lon stopped walking. His eyes widened. "No."

His stomach gurgled like it was filled with boiling tar. He shuffled to a spot between thick clumps of brush and exploded out his back end. The smell was instantaneous and so foul he gagged and vomited in front of him. His dog half went on a ravenous bender last night and he was paying the price. At least he assumed so, anyway. Everything burned.

Somewhere, not far off, a dog barked. An actual dog. Not like him. Well, as far as he knew anyway. His kind didn't typically transform during the day unless under increasingly stressful circumstances or near-death instances. He wasn't sure why it worked like that. Hell, he wasn't sure how anything worked if he were to be honest.

Once the cramps and nausea faded, he glanced around for something to clean up with and found nothing but pinecones, a scatter of dead leaves and a few mushrooms.

"Great," he said and reached for the scatter of leaves.

Maybe if he got a good portion of it he'd find a stream nearby to wash up better. The leaves proved not to work as he hoped they would, most of them falling out of his hand before he could wipe much of anything. He eyed the pinecones, shivered at what that would feel like and opted for the mushrooms. Which were large and white. Those worked better than the leaves but broke apart too easily.

By the end of it, he had more shit on his hand than the leaves or mushrooms.

Lon sighed and stood. He glanced around for more dead leaves or maybe some moss to clean up better. Eventually he found a small maple tree and pulled green leaves from it, which worked well enough and a bit farther on, he found a small patch of moss. Not perfect, but better than drying into a mat and attracting flies and whatever else.

He stumbled into a large clearing choked with tall, green grass. A ripple swam through the tall grass, though Lon didn't feel a breeze. He blinked and waited. The ripple didn't happen again. Maybe he imagined it, which was possible. His mind was waking up after being locked and subdued in the Old Man's care all to pad the bastard's pockets.

Lon thought about Max. The oldest of the Old Man's dog slaves. Max was trapped with the Old Man for over thirty years. Thirty goddamn years. Like a worker who should be seeking retirement. The Old Man retired Max, alright. But Max was a good man. A wise grandfather with a streak of humor. If not for Max, Lon wouldn't have made it.

"Ya gotta stand out, kid," Max said a couple months after Lon arrived at the compound with a few other boys, or what the Old Man called... pups. Max had been in the same room, though in different cages at the time. "If he takes a liken to ya, he won't completely starve ya. Let that dog part of ya learn it too. Every kill should be bloody and make the crowd cheer for more." He chuckled. "That's if ya wanna live, o'course. If not, then all ya gotta do is sit there and let the other one in that big ol'cage rip your throat out."

Death by ripped out throat didn't sound very appealing, so Lon took Max's advice and fought hard, creating the goriest shows, according to the Old Man, anyone had ever seen during the history of dog fights.

Once Lon was established as the Old Man's show runner, he put a bullet in Max's head and fed him to the pups.

While the past faded, Lon now ventured into the tall grass. It was almost as high as his shoulders, and he stood about six feet tall. Still, the deeper into the grass he went, the stranger he felt. Like something was watching him. Something in the grass…

His heart quickened, breath catching in his throat at the sound of slow, deliberate slithering coming not from one side, but all sides. He stopped, eyes shifting back and forth in their sockets. The slithering continued for a few seconds then fell silent. The tall grass whispered around him. It moved without any breeze at all.

He never trucked much with the paranormal. Ghosts. Demons. All that. Never truly experienced anything that proved those things existed. Supernatural was another story, of course. But…

Lon sprinted through the grass as fast as his legs would carry him and he could have sworn he heard something behind him. Something fast and hungry and ready to latch on to him. Ready to gorge itself on his flesh. Tiny shrieks filled his head and he stumbled, barely catching his balance, and launched himself the rest of the way out of the tall grass.

He landed on all fours and scrambled away from the grass as fast as he could.

Once in the forest again, he glanced back at the clearing. The tall grass appeared to shiver. Something hissed.

Heart thrumming, Lon turned and hurried away from the place. There was something in the clearing. Something, perhaps, paranormal?

Regardless, whatever it was… was hungry…

CHAPTER 7

IT WASN'T SO much a river than a long, muddy pond.

The water didn't flow like a river. Zero movement. Just a stagnant body of water that resembled a river, which stretched from left to right for as far as he could see. Frogs croaked and paint turtles lounged on partially submerged logs here and there. The water itself resembled chocolate milk in color. Probably nothing he wanted to wash his ass in either.

Did dogs like him get sick from bad water?

He didn't know and decided not to find out.

Still, his throat ached for a drink. How long had it been since he left the Old Man's place? A day? Something like that. Nothing to drink or eat since then. Never mind what the dog part of him gorged itself on and he later puked up. None of that was sustainable. He needed water and soon while living the human part of himself or he would die.

But not this water.

He walked downstream until he came to an old moss laden bridge. It reminded him of an old troll bridge from a fairytale book he read a long time ago. Or maybe his mother read it? He couldn't remember much of that life anymore. It was all muddled with blood and sharp teeth.

The bridge, made of wood, had to be at least fifty years old, as the thing bowed in the middle and the wood itself, that not festooned with moss, was black, gray, and cracked. Like old decaying bones.

The river, or whatever the long body of muddy water was below stank of something foul. A stench he was vaguely aware of, and now, closer, much worse. Maybe it was field runoff? Pig shit. Cow shit. Pesticides. All of it flowing to this point in the forest.

Lon sighed, gagged, and returned his attention to the old bridge. The weakest point was, of course the middle where it sagged, but if he could get close and jump over that point…

He stepped onto one of the planks, its texture spongy and grimy under his bare foot. The plank groaned. Tawny water rippled against a weed choked bank below. Lon drew in a breath and stepped fully onto the bridge, letting it hold his weight, which wasn't much. The Old Man nearly starved him to death for years. The bridge groaned some more but held. He blew out the pent-up breath and looked for another spot of the bridge that appeared not as rotten.

About two feet from the middle, he stopped and

glanced at the rails on either side. The one on the right was mostly broken and what remained was barely held together by moss. The left side appeared intact, though weathered quite a bit. Probably rotten. Still, it was the right side of the bridge he decided to try first. The rails were destroyed, but the planks seemed to be less saggy.

Lon, choosing his steps carefully, moved toward—

The wooden planks disintegrated under him, and he dropped into the muddy water below. And it was at this moment he realized... he didn't know how to swim.

He splashed and wailed. Foul water filled his mouth and he spat it out, coughing and choking and...

His feet came to a rest on the squishy bottom. The thrashing and splashing stopped. He blinked and stood. The water only came to about an inch under his nipples. Spitting out a tiny stick, or whatever it was, Lon chuckled.

Dumbass, he thought and realized he was about halfway across the river. He sloshed his way out of it and into the tall weeds taking up the bank. Once out of the muck and walked through the weeds onto a narrow dirt path.

Lon frowned. Bridges and paths meant people were nearby. Or used to be. He wasn't sure he wanted to meet anyone right now, though. Especially being naked and all.

Even so, he followed the path for a while until he stopped from an itch on the back of his leg. He scratched his leg and was about to keep walking when he noticed his fingers were covered in blood.

"What…"

Lon's gaze fell on his arm. His eyes widened. Three fat leeches squirmed on his forearm, just below the crook the elbow. He gasped and yanked them off. Each one left a tiny stream of blood behind. His blood. He stood there for a moment, staring at the three leeches writhing on the dirt trail. He shivered.

Then he felt another itch on his leg. Trembling, he looked down. A hard lump formed in his throat he barely choked down. He gagged and his vision blurred a bit. His legs wriggled with leeches. Heart a hammering mess, he scraped the leeches off his legs. His breathing was frantic, damn near hyperventilating. He didn't know why. They were just leeches, and he knew they couldn't really hurt him but…

Lon spent the next five minutes making sure all the leeches he brushed off were dying on the dirt path. He stomped on a few for good measure, popping their bodies like water blood-filled balloons.

A few minutes later, once he was sure he got all the leeches off him, Lon frowned at the trail ahead. It appeared to go on forever. What time was it? Noon? Early afternoon? How long had he been trudging through the forest? He glanced at the sky through the green canopy. It was bright blue, but he wasn't sure where the sun was. Not directly above, though.

His mind shifted away from the time of day to the grumble his stomach gave. Hunger and thirst drove everything else out of his mind. He needed both immediately, but water was the main priority.

He stared at the path. It was manmade. Like the bridge. Which meant people might be close by.

A shiver trickled through him, and he lurched forward. The forest wasn't providing what he needed… but people would. He dreamed of a garden hose as he walked the old trail away from the dilapidated bridge.

THE DOG FOUNDATION

RANDY WELLMAN, UP and coming oil tycoon behind his father, Rick Wellman, tossed a manila folder onto the glass table.

Some papers and a photo of the mark slid across the glass.

He shook his head and thought about the pack of cigarettes residing in the top center drawer of his desk. He quit ten years ago and rarely craved a smoke… but now…

Doug Tremp the only one at the table riding on his father's money and lucky realty deals rather than building an actual empire, reached out and slid the photo that escaped from the manila envelope closer to him. He tapped it.

"This is our top dog?" Doug grimaced. "Looks like a bitch I used to fuck back in Queens."

Everyone at the table shook their heads.

Randy rolled his eyes. "Doug, can you stop being a sick bastard for at least five minutes?"

Doug chuckled and leaned back in his chair. He messed with his obvious combover for a second or two and waved a dismissive hand. "Well get on with it then."

Randy sat at the head of the table, checked his phone and returned it to the inside pocket of his suit jacket. He regarded the seven people seated around the table. The Dog Foundation. Randy himself founded and funded the first dog fights before other like-minded, and wealthy, people wanted to join in and made it one of the most lucrative underground enterprises. Never in his wildest dreams had he realized how many werewolves ran around out there. He heard there were a few puppy mills out there that wanted to be sponsored too.

A venture he was seriously considering.

For now, though…

"Gentlemen," he said and gestured at the manilla folder. "I want you to meet Lon Crandle. Go ahead and pass it around."

Since it was closer to him, Doug gathered up the folder, slid the photo (the human part of Lon) aside and opened the folder.

"As you'll see for yourself," Randy said and leaned back in his chair. "Lon has been our top fighter, our highest sponsored dog, for a little over six years. He is undefeated."

"Well, yeah," Doug said in his weasely voice. "We wouldn't be talking about him if was defeated." He laughed his weird little laugh.

Randy sighed. Of all the people he wished he could send packing; it would be Doug Tremp. The guy was grotesquely annoying in every way. Uncultured and dimwitted. Still, the man helped bring revenue too, so…

"Right," Randy said as Doug slid the folder to the next man, Micheal Jules. Randy liked Mike. Quiet, but probably the man with most connections in the room.

"Anyway," Randy continued. "Lon Crandle has brought in more revenue than any other dog, including Max Devero. Who you all know was put down because of his age." Randy watched the folder get passed to the next man. Edward Mosk. Almost eighty and still a playboy. As wild as they come billionaire.

Randy stood and casually walked around the table. The meeting room wasn't anything special. Just a room with black tile and black walls. The far wall was stark white and used for projector slides and briefings. Something he almost used but decided a big production wasn't needed.

"If we lose Lon, we lose millions in revenue," he said and stopped at the other end of the table. The chair was empty, and he gripped the top of the backrest as he spoke. "We don't have another dog of his level to replace him. Gentlemen…" He straightened and slowly walked around the other side of the table. He paused behind Doug. "We will quite literally be fucked."

Everyone looked at him then. It wasn't often Randy swore and they knew if he did then something was seriously wrong.

Randy chuckled humorlessly and patted Doug's shoulder before moving on and sitting in his chair. He leaned forward, elbows on the table, fingers steepled in front of his face. His gaze drifted over the men seated around the table.

"We have reason to believe Lon will seek civilization." Randy leans back in his chair. It gives a gentle whoosh as he does. "If he survives the Chippewa Forest, the nearest town is over one hundred miles away."

"Won't the dog part keep him alive?" Jeff Baxter said. His bald head gleamed under the fluorescent light.

"Only at night," Randy said. "You should know that by now." He frowned at Jeff. "And, depending on what the dog part consumes, as we all know... it will be voided in the morning. So, Lon's stomach will be mostly empty, no matter how much the dog ate the night before. The human system cannot tolerate what a dog will eat."

Jeff nodded and looked at the folder in front of him. "So, what's the plan?"

"He shouldn't be hard to find," Micheal Jules said. He looked directly at Randy. "Send in a team and pick him up."

Randy smiled. He liked Micheal's idea, but...

"Or..." Randy shifted in his chair a bit. "We create a gameshow."

They gaped at him for a long time, and he reveled in the confusion. They were all very intelligent men, well, except for Doug, and catching them off guard gave Randy a bit of an erection, to be honest. It wasn't often you could surprise seasoned multibillionaires.

Randy chuckled. "That's right. We're going to expand and our very own Lon Crandle, our superstar, will lead the way."

Everyone stared at him, and he savored the moment.

"What do you mean gameshow?" Doug said. Not an entirely stupid question.

"We have four contestants hunt Lon over the course of three days. Whoever catches him will receive a grand prize." Randy shrugged. "Say a five million dollars."

Doug nodded, though Randy doubted if the dolt truly comprehended everything that was said.

"And if he kills them?" Micheal said.

Randy shrugged. "Then we cover it up and get four more contestants."

After a few minutes, Jeff shook his head. "I don't know. This sounds a bit too risky. Dogs killing each other is one thing, but when a dog kills a person…" He looked at Randy. "Are you thinking you want to broadcast this?"

"Not mainstream, of course," Randy said. "That would be insane. But I'm sure we can get Max and his techs to create a special broadcast signal to duck under FCC's radar and stream to a specific channel."

"We would need safeguards in place so the stream doesn't get leaked," Jeff said.

Randy nodded. "I'll talk to Max about all of that." He leaned back in his chair and gestured at them. "What do you all think about the concept?"

None of them spoke for a long time. Doug

brought out his phone and fiddled with it a bit before stuffing it back into the inside pocket of his jacket. Micheal crossed his arms over his chest and frowned at the table. Jeff shook his head and sighed. The other did everything except look at Randy.

"Well?" Randy said. "You're all very quiet now."

"I think it's a good idea," Jeff said after a few seconds. "But I'm not sure if the payout is worth the risk."

Randy chuckled. "Remember when we were getting the fights and Dog Foundation off the ground? The possibility of leaks and all that? This is about the same."

"Not exactly," Micheal said. "The fights and organization aren't being broadcasted or streamed. Whatever it is now. Less exposure and easier to hide."

"I say we go for it," Edward Mosk said. He glanced around the table at each man. "If it gets leaked, how will they trace it to any of us?" He ran a hand through his wispy white hair and smiled. His perfectly straight teeth glimmered. "Dog Foundation is protected by over a million dummy foundations. They could try to trace it to us, but they would fail." He stood and pointed at Randy. "I'm with Randy on this. We run this little gameshow until we get a fighter like Lon fully trained and ready."

Randy smiled and, gradually, the other men smiled too.

CHAPTER 8

IT WAS AROUND dusk when Lon staggered to the edge of the forest.

He stared at the empty blacktop road and his heart sank. He had hoped to find a town or house where he could get a drink from a garden hose or something. Anything. All he knew was he needed water. Badly. There wasn't even a pond or stream from what he could see. Just the blacktop winding away into what could be another damn forest.

Lon shivered and glanced at the sky. It was summer, so the daylight lasted longer, but his bones told him the change was coming soon. And what then? He would take a backseat while the dog part of him ran free.

He just hoped nobody would get hurt.

He stepped out of the forest into a thick patch of weeds and wildflowers. Bees and butterflies buzzed and flitted from bloom to bloom. The air was sweet and green and soothing. The heat of the day was already tapering off, giving way to a gentler evening. He stood among the weeds and flowers and bees and butterflies and sweet air and smiled. How long had it been since he smiled? Truly smiled? How long had it been since he was happy?

Lon, still smiling, stepped out of the patch of weeds and flowers and onto the blacktop. The asphalt was warm under his bare feet. He glanced up and down the road. There were no signs. A raccoon, long dead, lay bloated up the road a bit. Fat black flies covered the thing.

He decided to walk down the road rather than in the direction of the dead raccoon. He walked on the road instead of the gravely shoulder. The rocks hurt his feet too much. Birds sang from the trees on either side of the road. A hawk darted from one canopy to the other. Frogs croaked in the deep ditches as he walked by. Ditches filled with cattails.

The road sloped gently downward, making the walk easier. It was still light out, but not as bright as it should be. During the summer, night typically eased its way in to snuff out the day. That's how he remembered it anyway. Too many memories were wiped away when he was bitten years ago. There were vague wisps of memories that would float within his dreams. Ghosts. If they were real memories or not, he didn't know.

He was about halfway down the gentle hill when something caught his left peripheral vision. He stopped walking and turned. At first, he wasn't sure what he was looking at. His heart thudded. His breathing slowed. Lon squinted and…

"W… Water…" His voice was barely above a croak.

Lon swayed. Through the trees the glistening water of a lake stole all of his attention. He walked across the road, through a swamping ditch and into a wooded area like a zombie. Driven by only one need. His bare feet slid through a blanket of dead pine needles, more than a few sticking into the soles and toes of his feet. He ignored the pain. He ignored everything. His throat screamed for water. His body cried. His mind was set securely into survival mode.

He shuffled onto a beach of tawny sand littered with washed up reeds and clam shells. He kicked through the sand and sloshed into the lake up to his thighs. He dropped to his knees, relishing the cool of the lake washing away all the dirt and grime and blood. Washing away everything. Maybe even his sins? He dunked himself under and shook his head back and forth. The water around him turned murky with all the filth.

Once he rinsed himself off and was cooled down a bit, he moved deeper into the lake. Up to his chin. He snorted as small fish nibbled at his legs.

Then he took a sip of lake water. But the sip wasn't enough. He slurped up more water. He drank. He gulped. He couldn't stop. The thirst was all that mattered. He drank deeply from the lake.

It wasn't until his stomach began churning when he wondered if drinking from the lake was a bad thing…

He managed to back up a few steps before he

vomited up all the water he had just consumed. He thrashed backward while lake water vomited out of him. He fell onto the beach, burping up the rest of the water he drank. He gagged up bile and groaned. Maybe he drank it too fast? Or maybe… a memory slithered into his mind just then. Something he learned at a young age. You needed to boil lake water because of all the bacteria and pathogens floating around in it.

"Damn," he managed and rolled onto his side.

Small waves lapped at his feet. He shivered and closed his eyes. He couldn't keep going. There was nothing left in him now.

Lon curled up into a ball on the beach as night gradually consumed him.

CHAPTER 9

IT WAS THE scent that woke him.

A sweet, meaty scent.

Lon's muzzle twitched. His nostrils flared, drawing in more of the delicious scent. The human part of Lon was sleeping now. Too weak to be conscious.

The dog part of him had full control. At least for now.

Lon the dog stood on his hind legs and glanced around. He didn't know where he was and wondered why he wasn't in his room. He blinked at the lake and the moonlight glistening off its surface.

He stepped into the lake, bent, and lapped up a few deep slurps of water. Then that scent caught his attention again. Lon rose. Water dripped from the fur of his lower jaw as he sniffed the air. So fresh! More and more scents mingle with the sweet meaty one that woke him up. Animals. Deer. Skunks. Raccoons. Frogs. There was also something with a feline stench. Not exactly a cat but something larger. Could be a problem, but he wasn't too concerned.

He walked away from the lake and focused on the sweet meaty scent. He drew it in. He savored the taste on the back of his tongue. The scent lured him across the road and into a wooded area that wasn't quite a forest. Lon followed it until he came to an alfalfa field. Which irritated his sinuses, and he lost the scent.

Sneezes exploded out of him as he ran on all fours around the field and into more woods. Once he was away from the alfalfa, he stood on his hind legs again and sniffed the air. He lost the scent and needed to...

There.

Lon found the delicious scent again and followed it through a valley and turkey farm. He grabbed a turkey for the road, ravaged it, and feathers trailed behind him. He ran undistracted through more woods, a cornfield, until finally skidded to a stop on the outskirts of town.

He crept behind a thicket and took in the scent. It was so close now but there were people in towns. People meant danger. Master taught him that. Never trust people. Only trust Master. But Master wasn't here. Which meant no punishments. And with no punishments...

Relief spilled through Lon the dog. He trembled with something near to ecstasy. He was free. Finally... free. Something he never thought he'd feel.

The sweet meaty scent shoved everything else out of his mind. His stomach growled. The hunger. It was always the hunger. Hunger is what drove him. Sometimes he could think around it but more often than not… the hunger won.

He slunk into the town keeping to the deepest shadows. Except for the streetlights, the town appeared to be asleep. But appearances were deceiving. Like the scent. Why was it so alluring? Why did it demand…

Once Lon moved deeper into the town, he spotted why the scent was so strong.

A big man in a black ball cap and a black and yellow jersey stood on his small porch tending to the various meats he cooked on his grill. Shellfish like lobster and shrimp and… yes… there was steak in there. Beef. The scent was a mingling of all the scents, including the cook's sweat.

Saliva filled his mouth and drooled down the front of his lower jaw. He watched the man flip the steaks, shut the grill lid and went into the house.

Lon rushed forward, seizing on the opportunity to get the steaks and…

The man stepped outside just as Lon entered the yard and suddenly, he didn't care about the steaks anymore. Master taught him hurting people was bad, but the man on the porch was so large. His sweat glistened on his face like a glaze. His blood. Lon could smell the man's blood. The man's heartbeat invaded Lon's ears and pummeled into his brain.

He leaped over the hedge running along the side of the porch, used the porch's railing to spring off and pounced onto the man. The man managed a squeal before Lon's teeth ripped his flabby throat out. Blood spurted and Lon clamped his mouth over the fount. He drank deeply for a few seconds then sank his teeth in and shook his head. He tore a larger chunk out of the man's throat and swallowed it down.

The man writhed sluggishly. Like someone drowning. His exposed esophagus made weak slurping sounds. And, even with most of his throat gone, he tried crawling into his house. He managed to get about halfway across the threshold.

Lon grunted, bent down, grasped the man's head in both claws, and yanked the jowly head from the large body. Lon tossed the head aside and tore into the man's back. He clawed out the kidneys and relished the way they kind of popped in his mouth when he chewed them. He chewed on the spinal cord, snapping it and drinking the fluid.

Somewhere in his mind Master was calling him a bad dog. A very bad dog. But that old voice was far away. Master didn't matter anymore. He was a free dog now.

Blood pooled around Lon and the man's corpse. It splattered the glass porch door, the grill, the porch, all over the tiles inside the house near the door. Blood was everywhere, which fed Lon's frenzy. The sweet scent of blood.

He rolled the corpse over and ripped into the bulging stomach. He tore away the gobbets salty fat and gulped it down. He sucked down the intestines, cracked the ribcage and pried it open. Lon bit into the heart when a scream broke through his frenzy.

He blinked. His gaze lifted away from the corpse to a young girl no older than ten.

The very sight woke the human part of Lon up. There was a bit of a duality at first, but the human part won. He dropped the heart and forced the dog part of him to leave. He stumbled into the grill and knocked it over. Burnt steaks and lobster tails spilled out on to the porch. Lon leaped into the back yard and raced into the night.

The taste of human blood was still on his tongue.

CHAPTER 10

IT WAS DIFFICULT as hell with claws, but Lon managed to turn the water spigot on the outside of a snoozing house and drink his fill. Once he puked up all the nastiness the dog part ate, he would need to drink more water. But, for now at least, he was hydrated.

He turned in the direction of the house he fled. Where the dog part killed and ate a man. A father. The girl's screams still haunted him. Lon blamed himself for not being strong enough to be aware and keep the dog part from going rogue like that. He also wished he could give that girl her father back. Seeing all the blood, the headless, gutless corpse with its chest pried open and a literal monster feasting on her father's heart...

Lon fought the dog part off for a bit and snuck into a house where someone forgot to lock the back door. He needed clothes. The laundry room, fortunately, was in the basement of this household. Unfortunately, there wasn't much in the dryer except for baby and kids' clothes.

He growled and hurried out of the house.

At another house he came across where everyone was asleep, he found a pair of men's jeans that looked like they might fit and a pair of black work boots. He stowed the jeans and boots in an old shed on the outskirts of town and darted back to town for more clothing.

It was at a quaint ranch style house where he stuck the mother load. The laundry room, also fortunately in the basement, had not only a full basket of clothes, but a dryer too. The clothes were obviously from an older couple, but Lon found a pair of underwear that would fit, socks, and a couple of shirts.

He crept toward the back door to leave when he wondered what they could spare to eat.

In the kitchen, he grabbed the loaf bread right away. He took a couple cans of chicken noodle soup and hurried toward the backdoor again.

A throaty growl stopped him at the door.

He turned around to find another dog, though not like him, staring at him. It bared its teeth, growl rising in volume.

Lon snorted and exited the house without further issue. The dogs not like him were more bark than bite most of the time.

He stored the clothes, bread and cans of chicken noodle soup in the old shed and stumbled a bit outside. He wanted to get a jug of water or something but the human part of him was beginning to fade again. He struggled as long as he could but was too weak to hold on.

The dog part reemerged.

Lon blinked and glanced around. He didn't like the human part when it tried to control him. They were the same, yet not at all. Like identical twins. He sniffed the air and found not only the scent of blood from the man on the porch, but something else…

That feline stench…

Not a cat. Not exactly. But something very similar. Something larger.

And it was close.

Lon slipped into the deeper shadows of a nearby barn and waited.

The feline was obviously hunting him. It was used to easier prey, though. Nothing like him.

He crouched behind an old broken-down tractor and peered through the space between the steering wheel, shifter, and floor.

Its stench was getting stronger. Nauseating.

A mild breeze tickled the fur on his left arm. He shifted a bit to not be downwind from the rank feline. His mind drifted to the child. The screaming child whose father's heart he ate. He thought about returning to that house. A family. Maybe he would eat them all…

Lon shook his head to focus on the large feline stalking him. Good thing he did because it slunk out of the shadows near the shed and stopped. It seemed like it was glowing under the moonlight. He watched it look around, searching for him. Then it turned to the shed. The door was left open.

Being downwind, it couldn't smell him, but he could smell it.

He waited for the large feline to turn away and he shot across the space between the barn and the shed on all fours. He was only a few feet away before the feline heard him and spun around.

Too late.

Lon slammed into the animal and bashed its head against the ground. It tried scrambling free and raked him with its sharp claws. Lon grabbed one of the front legs and snapped it like a twig. The feline shrieked and tried to flee but he sank his own claws into its back and drug it closer. It once more slashed and bit him. Lon roared, picked the animal up and slammed it onto the ground three times and tossed it into the nearest tree. Its body bounced off the tree trunk and landed hard in a patch of weeds.

It tried to move but, in the end, collapsed. It laid in the weeds, sides expanding and deflating with every labored breath. Tiny mewls escaped the feline.

Lon growled deep in his throat and ate his fill.

THE DOG FOUNDATION

"WE'RE READY TO rock," Max Williams said and swiveled his chair around to face Randy.

"It's set up to stream on the correct channel?"

"Yup," Max said and smiled. "When are you planning on streaming?"

Randy thought it over for a bit and shrugged. "In the next day or so, I think. We need contestants and a host."

"Should we alert the town's mayor and authorities?"

Randy chuckled and shook his head. "No." He lit a cigar and puffed on it thoughtfully for a few seconds. He pointed the cigar at Max. "It'll make for a good show if no one knows what's going on." He grinned. "Nothing like real, visceral reactions to catch the audience's reaction." He didn't mention the special surprise that was already dropped off near the town.

Max nodded slowly. "I guess that makes sense."

Randy snorted, patted the side of Max's shoulder. "Of course it does. This is entertainment, kid."

"Sure," Max said and frowned a bit. "People are going to get killed on a live stream." It wasn't a question.

Randy liked the kid. Max was extremely intelligent and knew all the ins and outs of the tech world. He was intuitive and loyal. But sometimes he popped off with statements that pissed Randy off.

"Your job," Randy said and jabbed the stogie at Max. "Is to make sure the stream stays live and undetected." He bent so that he stared directly into Max's eyes. "Do your job… and I'll do mine."

Max gulped and nodded. His voice was small and weak. "Understood."

CHAPTER 11

THE SINGING WOKE HIM.

Not actual singing but something lighter and not very complex. Something familiar.

Birds?

Lon's eyes fluttered opened and his gaze fixed on the spill of sunlight like fresh honey over his bloodstained wrist. A shiver racked his body. He swallowed and his throat made a thick, dry click. His stomach gurgled. Every muscle screamed when he moved. His head throbbed as he rolled onto his back and stared at the ceiling. A ceiling with its rafters filled with spare two by fours, scraps of drywall, miscellaneous strips of house siding and random garden tools like rakes, shovels, and hoes.

A violent shiver struck him like a dull awakening.

He coughed and rolled around trying to find water. But there wasn't any water. He didn't get a chance to collect any before fading last night. He crawled to the soup cans. It wasn't water, but they had liquid so maybe…

"Shit," he croaked, realizing he forgot to grab a can opener.

He dropped the soup can shuffled toward the door of the shed. It was hot in there and reeked of gasoline and oil. The floorboards groaned under his weight, such as it was. Sweat trickled down his face and the small of his back. He glanced at the wadded bundle of clothes he stole and didn't want to put them on. It was that hot. He opened the door a crack and squinted at the bright sunlight until his eyes got used to it.

The shed was nestled near an old barn and a dilapidated house. He couldn't see anything else through the crack so opened it a bit more. The sun baked into his skin. A wooded area filled his left peripheral. Straight ahead, through a yard choked with weeds, was what appeared to be a road or street.

Other than all of that… he was out in the middle of nowhere as far as he could tell.

His gaze shifted to the old, dilapidated house. Most of the roof looked like it had caved in. But…

Lon's focus narrowed on the red yard hydrant between the barn and house.

Not a hand pump but one of those hydrants that was more like a spigot. A direct line to the well and when you pulled the red handle, well water would shoot out. One of those vague, ghostly memories waved in front of his mind's eye. An image of a hydrant with a red handle just like the one across the way.

He opened the door and stepped outside. He glanced around, but it appeared the little homestead was the only one around. One side was dominated by a cornfield while trees loomed over the other side. A small, wooded area. Or a forest. Lon wasn't sure and didn't care right now. He staggered to the yard hydrant with the chipped, red handle.

Lon swallowed and his throat made a dry click. His vision was getting blurry now. He grabbed the handle, which was warm from the morning sun, and pulled it up. It squealed from the rust around the joint.

The hydrant made a glugging sound but didn't shoot out any water.

"No," Lon said in a raspy voice. He gripped the sides of his head and trembled. "No, no, no!" He punched the red head of the hydrant and roared. He punched it again. And again.

Blood smeared the handle and spigot from his split knuckles.

Lon dropped to his knees in the weeds. A few spooked grasshoppers flicked away from him. The sobs that racked his weakened body quaked every organ. He slumped... defeated. He was going to die and maybe that was for the best. Maybe—

The hydrant burped up orange water.

He sucked in a sharp breath and crawled closer to the spigot. Another burp of orange water spewed onto the tall grass. Glugging sounds came from the pipe. Lon tore away some of the grass and sucked the water droplets from the blades.

The hydrant groaned and Lon wasn't sure if the

damn thing was going to explode or not.

Then water blasted out of the spigot with so much force it flattened the tall grass in front of his.

A giggle slipped out of Lon's mouth. Still giggling, he crawled under the blast of water. It was cold and wet, and the best thing Lon had felt in a long time. A pool soon formed around the hydrant and Lon laid face down in the muddy water for a few seconds, savoring it. Then he turned and tried to take a drink from the spigot, but the water pressure was way too high.

On trembling legs, he stood, sloshed through the muddy water and lowered the hydrant's handle until it was a steady stream. Then he bent and slurped down the water. He drank deeply. It was cold and wet and that's all his body needed. Lon stopped himself from drinking too much too fast, remembering something the Old Man said.

"Don't drink it too fast, ya damn pup! Y'll puke it all but up."

Lon shivered and instead of drinking, decided to wash the dirt and blood off his body. He already felt one hundred percent better. He shut the hydrant off and walked around the property a bit to dry off. The heat of the sun soaked into the top of his head and shoulders.

If he was going to make this his home, at least for now, he needed to know the area. Just in case something crazy happened. He walked around the house to the front. The front yard was surrounded by a picket fence that might have been white at one time but now resembled gray rib bones. Some of the posts were broken or missing. A couple of old oaks dominated the left and right of the house. The entire front yard was choked with weeds and saplings. Beyond the front yard was a paved road that appeared to stretch forever from the left but sloped gently into a small town surrounded by woods.

Despite being small, the town appeared to sprawl far and wide. Looks could be deceiving though.

His stomach gurgled and he turned around. The house slumped in front of him like a broken beast. A warm breeze soothed his damp skin. Most of the windows were broken or missing completely. Slivers of glass twinkled in the weeds below the missing windows. One side of the roof had caved in at one point or another. The siding, which might have been white in its prime, was now gray and splintered.

Lon walked around the house to the back yard again. He spotted a mangled corpse covered in flies of something near the shed and walked to the old barn instead of investigating. The barn, while old, appeared to be in good shape. He opened the large front doors. The rusty hinges popped like gunshots, startling Lon. His heart thrummed. He shook his head and opened the doors the rest of the way. They gave a loud squawk that echoed throughout the barn.

An old milking barn, by the look of it. A four-foot breezeway. A concrete path with milking stalls on either side. The barn smelled vaguely of manure and sour milk, but all of that was subdued by the musty aroma of elderly hay. The rusty stalls were caked with bird shit, as well as the breezeway. He wanted to look through the building more. Maybe there were supplies he could use, but his stomach screamed for food.

Lon shut the barn doors and walked to the shed.

The mangled, fly infested corpse lay twisted not far from the shed. Blood stained the weeds and grass around it. Fat, black flies buzzed lazily around the mess. It stank, but not as bad as it would in a couple more hours. He didn't know what it used to be but knew his dog part was responsible. He sighed and went on a search around the area for something to remove the corpse without touching it. The important thing was to move the mess as far away from the shed as he could so it wouldn't attract bears or anything else. The less attention, the better.

The Old Man and the others were surely out there looking for him. He was the star, after all.

After a while, he found a rust laden pitchfork with a gray, broken wooden handle behind the barn. He scooped up the corpse, which was large enough to be heavy and appeared to be some kind of animal judging by the patches of fur twisted among tendons and shreds of meat and bone. Its head was missing, which made identifying the thing nearly impossible.

He dumped the mutilated animal as far as he could in the woods and covered it with dead branches.

Lon walked back to the shed, stabbed the rusty pitchfork into the ground and stepped into the sweltering shed. He sifted through the clothes, slipped on underwear, jeans and t-shirt. He was about to put on the boots and realized he didn't have socks.

"Damn," he said and forced his sweaty feet into the boots.

Then he went back outside to get away from the heat in the shed. The breeze was warm but cooler than being in that old hotbox. Lon drank some more water and sat in the shade until the sun lowered a bit and listened to the birdsong dwindle. It was the most peace he ever had.

Once it got a little cooler, Lon ventured back to the shed and opened the bread. He grabbed a few slices and walked back outside, stomach aching for food. He slowly ate one of the slices. No matter how much he wanted to scarf it down, he managed to eat it small piece by small piece. One could say the Old Man was a bad man, but he taught Lon some fundamental survival tactics. Don't drink too fast or too much if you're dehydrated. Don't eat too fast if you're starving.

He would need more than bread, but right now… he savored the bread.

By the time dusk seeped in, Lon ate four slices of bread and drank enough water to where he could relax a bit more. He needed to find a can opener for the chicken noodle soup. He yawned and looked at the shed. If he was going to make this place his home, he at least needed a bed of some sort.

He began walking toward the shed and collapsed into a patch of thick weeds.

CHAPTER 12

Lon WOKE TO the orchestra of crickets and frogs.

He stood, frowning with his dog's eyes. The stench of the dead feline drew him toward the woods. If not for the human part, it would have finished eating the corpse.

The human part of Lon, which was far more alert than last night, sent the dog part to town. He needed a can opener, socks, maybe some blankets and a pillow, and more food. A cup and bowl would be great too. The dog part tried to fight him a bit, but eventually let the human part lead.

For now, at least.

The town was much larger than it looked from the homestead up the hill. Lon crept in the shadows. It was night, but not many homes were dark. Which led him to believe he was in a later month like August or September. Where the weather is still relatively hot in the Midwest, though the days begin to get shorter. Nightfall around eight-thirty or nine o'clock, full darkness around ten. Busy families still up getting kids to bed and such, he assumed. Maybe a few night owls.

Eventually he found a house with all its lights off.

He snuck to the back door and suddenly he was trapped in bright light. A light above the back door spotlighted him. A motion light. A dog not like him barked from inside the house. A man told it to shut up.

Lon leaped out of the light, climbed over a wooden fence, and sprinted away from the house. Several minutes later, he was about to enter a different house when he caught a strange, yet familiar scent. He blinked and turned away from the house. His gaze floated toward a thicket not far from the backyard. It was in there. Could it be another dog like him? If so, something was off about it. He drew in the scent and lowered to all fours. He moved toward the thicket. The closer he got, the stronger the scent.

Then the breeze shifted and blew toward the thicket. Lon stopped. Sniffed. He lost the scent.

Eventually the breeze shifted again, but the scent had vanished.

Lon snorted and looked around slowly. Something was out there. Something like him, yet… not entirely.

He turned back to the house, found a can opener, a pair of jeans, socks and—

A small gasp stopped him. Stopped him cold. He almost dropped all the items in his arm. The dog part of him clawed at his psyche to be free. Lon wouldn't be able to hold it for much longer. It wanted to run.

Lon, in dog form, turned around to find a boy, no older than twelve with shaggy brown hair, gaping at him. The boy stumbled back a bit when Lon shifted from one hind leg to the other.

"D-Did you take my friend?" Tears trembled in his eyes. "Did you take all my friends?" The tears broke free and spilled down his cheeks. "Give them back. Please give them back." He stepped forward. "Y-You can take me instead. Just… just let them go. Please."

A growl gurgled in his throat, and he choked it down before he really terrified the kid.

Moving quickly, he left the house and ran into the darkness.

Behind him, the boy sobbed.

CHAPTER 13

HE DUMPED THE can opener and clothes in the shed and managed to make it a few feet away before the dog part finally clawed its way through.

Lon the dog shivered and blinked. He sniffed the air but there weren't any scents he wanted to investigate. The night was alive with all kinds of sounds he never heard while in his room. Those dirty concrete walls…

But here he was. Free. Finally, and there was nothing more he could ever want right n—

A faint scream snatched his attention. He sprinted on all fours toward town and stopped not far from the homestead. He listened for a bit and the scream found his pointy ears again. A bit louder this time. His heart thudded. A deep growl filled his throat and Lon raced in the direction of the scream.

He skidded to a stop in the town's park. Which

was rather large and dotted with picnic tables and shelters for parties and gatherings. Most of the shelters had various flyers of missing children tacked to them like grotesque wallpaper.

The playground took up a big chunk of the park. He sniffed the air, catching all kinds of scents, but nothing really piqued his interest. His hearing caught all kinds of voices and sounds. Babies crying. A man shouting. A few dogs, not like, him barked or growled. Cats, those disgusting felines, hissing and meowing. The crickets and frogs. Children laughing—

Then he caught a whiff of blood. Faint, but there floating on a rogue breeze. Drool seeped into the fur of his chin. It was human blood. Blood Master told him not to drink. He followed the scent before the breeze changed. It led him to a small house at the end of a dead-end street. There were no streetlights, and the house was consumed in darkness. With his dog's eyes he was able to see clearly enough.

The front door of the house was broken in. Torn off the hinges and nothing but a twisted chunk of metal on the stoop. Whatever did that was extremely strong.

Lon drew in the air before approaching. The scent of blood was strong… but there was something else. Something hiding under the blood. A thick musk. A dog like him, but its scent was strange and confused Lon a bit. There was something else mixed in with the scent. Something that twisted Lon's gut, though he couldn't name or recognize the scent.

The mingling scent was completely alien to Lon.

His heart thrummed as he moved forward on all-fours, head lowered. His gaze shifted back and forth, up and down, searching for any movement. His nostrils flared, taking in every scent he could.

The closer he got to the doorway, the faster his heart thumped.

The Dog Foundation

"Hello, hello," Rodney Quinn shouted as he stepped onto the stage. Behind him was a massive theater screen.

"How'd you get Rodney Quinn?" Jeff Baxter said as The Dog Foundation watched the show from the greenroom of the studio.

Randy poured himself a scotch and sat in a comfy. "Minor expense." He took a sip of his scotch.

"Welcome to the show you'll never forget," Rodney said as he walked from one end of the stage to the other. He stopped and smiled, lights playing off his perfectly straight, perfectly white teeth and blue eyes. His dark hair was swept back and shimmered as he moved.

All of it was Rodney Quinn's appeal. He oozed charisma and charm. Older women loved him. His voice was loud, booming, with a tinge of gruffness. His skin was a flawless tan.

Randy grunted as the man on stage pointed at the audience and shouted, "Are you ready?"

The audience roared in reply. Whistles and claps peppered the noise.

"Oh," Edward Mosk said. "He's good."

The rest of the Dog Foundation nodded in concurrence, which pleased Randy. He dumped a lot of money into this gameshow scheme. If it failed, however, he'd be out more than money. There would be a good chance the others would kick him out of the Foundation and cut him out of the business. He would have his oil business, but that shit wasn't fun.

It'll be a hit, Randy thought and sipped his scotch. *Please, fuck, let it be a hit.*

"Alright, ladies and gentlemen," Rodney Quinn said and slowly walked toward the other side of the stage. The spotlight followed him. "I know you're new here so here's the rub." He stopped walking and beamed a bright smile at the audience. "You vote for the hunter you think will be best take down the dog." He paused, smiled and walked to center stage. The audience was completely silent. "The first one to enter their vote and the hunter wins…"

Rodney nodded. "And the first person to vote for the correct hunter…" He paused again and Randy chuckled. Rodney Quinn was the best. Randy sipped more of his scotch.

"The very first person to vote for the correct hunter will win…" Rodney smiled. "They will win five *million* dollars!" He pointed at an older woman in the front row with short, curly hair. The spotlight fixed on her. She smiled and clutched her purse.

"Well, hello, darlin'," Rodney said and stepped off the stage and helped the woman to her feet. "What's your name, beautiful?"

The old woman giggled and kind of snuggled into Rodney. "Lisa."

Rodney grinned and wrapped an arm around her. "Well, hi, Lisa! You're so great. So great." He spoke to the top of her head. "Do you know who we're hunting today?"

Lisa blinked and looked up at Rodney. "Is it Lon Crandel?"

"Yes!" Rodney pointed at the giant theater screen above the stage.

On it was Lon winning several dog fights. A voiceover thundered throughout the studio.

"Lon Crandel. Fifty-time dog fight champion. The strongest dog to fight in an arena." The video switches to Lon tearing apart a security guard. "But some dogs can't be tamed."

The audience gasped.

"He didn't kill anyone when he escaped, though," Doug Tremp said.

"He didn't," Randy said, smiled and sipped his scotch. He leaned back in the chair. "Some minor editing to excite the audience."

The room fell silent as they watched, and Randy smiled again.

The video moved on to Lon escaping into the woods.

"Lon Crandel," the voiceover said. "He has escaped and is rampaging through the small town

of Dyer. Women and children... slaughtered."
Images of mutilated women and children, mostly
children, flashed across the screen and the audience
gasped again. Someone began sobbing.

"But there is hope," the voiceover continued, and
strong inspiring music rose in volume. "It is up to
you to save the residents of Dyer. Only you can stop
the carnage."

On the screen, a video of a few men and women
in tactical training and hunting dangerous predators
like tigers, lions and grizzly bears.

"You can choose the hunter to take down the
rogue dog," the voiceover boomed. "You have the
power."

The lineup of five hunters stood on the screen.
All of them holding a weapon of some kind. One
man held a chainsaw.

From the viewing room, Randy blinked. They
were supposed to go through all five hunters'
profiles and experience. He sighed and instead of
sipping the scotch, he slugged the rest back. Max
fucked up. Hopefully it wouldn't matter.

"Holy Moley" Rodney Quinn said and turned to
Lisa. "Now, Lisa..." He paused to build obvious
tension. "What you saw was pretty scary, right?
Women and children..." He tipped the microphone
toward her.

"Y... Yes." She rummaged through her purse.
"Pardon me. I need my inhaler."

Rodney, ever the professional, redirected for a bit
and drew attention to the three men and two
women on the screen above the stage. "Look at
them up there! Our brave hunters! Which one

would you choose? Which one can stop the strongest dog in the world?"

Randy grunted. That was good. He got another glass of scotch.

Once Lisa was done with her inhaler, Rodney spotlighted her again.

"So, my beautiful Lisa," Rodney said and beamed his bright smile at the camera. Lisa giggled. "Who do *you* think will save the women and children of Dyer?"

"Oh, I don't know," Lisa said and hugged her purse to her chest.

Rodney chuckled and pointed at the screen. "Well, you have five able bodied hunters up there, darlin'." He leaned close to Lisa, microphone between them. "Would it help if you knew their names?"

Lisa smiled. "Yes, it would."

"Well," Rodney said and swept a hand at the people on the screen. "Left to right, here we go. The big bald man there, with his elephant gun, is Bram. Now, right next to him is Kelly with her crossbow. And that soldier standing beside her is Sam, with his revolvers and Em with her uzis." Rodney flashed a smile and pointed at the last person on the screen. "And that man right there at the end is Will, one of the greatest snipers of all time."

The audience erupted in applause.

In the media room, Randy grunted and drank more scotch.

Once the audience's applause died down, Rodney hugged Lisa with one arm while the looked at the screen of hunters.

"So, Lisa," Rodney said in a quieter tone. Something almost mischievous. "Out of all five of our brave hunters… which one has your vote?" The sound of ticking clock echoed throughout the studio.

Lisa, mouth opened a bit, looked left to right, right to left. "Umm…"

A sharp ding startled Lisa and Rodney laughed. "Time's up, darlin'. Which hunter did you pick?"

Lisa shook her head, frowned and looked at Rodney. "I… I think I'm going to go with Bram."

"Big Bram," Rodney shouted and the audience applauded. He kissed the side of Lisa's head. "Thank you, Lisa!" He stepped back onto the stage. "It's up to you fine Americans now!" Numbers appeared above the Hunters' heads. Bram was number 1 and the numbers ranged to Will at 5.

"There are devices attached to the seats in front of you," Rodney said. "If you've ever visited a dog fight, you know how to use them. For everyone else, just tap the number that represents your hunter! That's it! Your votes will be tallied at the end of the program." Rodney paused and let his smile glimmer in the spotlight for a moment. "And the first person who voted for the correct hunter will win the grand prize of… *five million dollars*!"

The audience went wild for a few seconds until Rodney quieted them down.

"Now," Rodney said. "I want you all, at the count of three, to pick up those devices and place your vote. You too, Lisa." He winked at the old woman but the camera didn't show her reaction.

In a low, soothing voice, Rodney said, "Are you

ready?" He waited while the cameras skimmed over the audience while they picked up the voting devices on the chairs in front of them. People in the front row took their devices from a small, metal column in front of them.

Rodney grinned. "Here we go folks. Tap your vote on three." He paused a bit while people settled in. "Ready? Here we go now." He walked casually back and forth across the stage. "One... two..." He looked directly at the camera and smiled. "Three."

Randy polished off his third scotch and waited for the show to play out. There needed to be a few tweaks here and there for more episodes, but it was still an entertaining pilot.

A hand fell on his shoulder and a voice whispered in his ear. "We have a drone on Crandel."

Randy blinked. "Transmit stream to the media room."

"Yes, sir, I will—"

"Not the live stream," Randy added.

"Of course. The footage will be transmitted in two minutes."

Randy adjusted himself in the chair, which might as well been a recliner. The TV flickered.

"I think something is interrupting the stream," Micheal said.

"We have a drone on Lon," Randy said as the TV switched to a house seen through green tinged night vision.

"Oh," Doug said, nearly bouncing in his chair like a child. "This should be good!"

Randy rolled his eyes. God, he hated that man.

The drone moved around but, so far, there was no sign of Lon.

"Maybe he's in the house," Jeff said.

Randy drank his scotch and watched the drone move closer to the house.

CHAPTER 14

THE STENCH OF the other dog overwhelmed the sweet smell of blood the deeper Lon crept into the house.

Speaking of blood… it was everywhere. Splatters littered the floor, and the walls were covered in splashes.

He found the woman in a bedroom. The bed itself was torn apart and drenched in blood. It was then he discovered it wasn't just the woman, but two children too. Lon blinked and his human part reemerged. There was nearly nothing left of the bodies, they were so mutilated. Lon had been aware shortly before emerging. Another dog did this.

Its scent was so strong he gagged. Not just its musk but its piss. Which was all over the corpses and bedroom. It marked its territory. Its food. Which meant, if it wasn't in the house it would return.

Lon quietly left the room and searched the house for the other dog. The stench of its piss messed with Lon's senses. Too strong and covering up other scents. After a quick search, Lon hurried out of the house.

THE DOG FOUNDATION

LON RAN OUT of the house and almost plowed into the drone.

Randy jumped, almost spilling his drink. He chuckled a bit. No one in the room seemed to notice. Which was alright.

He was just about to sip more scotch when the drone caught movement on the roof of the .house. Randy lowered the glass and sat forward. His eyes widened.

Another dog crawled across the roof and stared off in the direction Lon ran.

Everyone on in the media room seemed to suck in a breath at the same time.

The dog, which appeared larger than Lon, stared for a few seconds, then its head turned, and it grinned at the drone.

"Oh, shit," Edward said.

The dog sprang from the roof at the drone and suddenly the screen went blank.

The Dog Foundation sat in silence for a while. Processing what they just saw. Randy, for one, was left speechless and knocked back the rest of his scotch.

Eventually, it was Doug, that bastard, who spoke first. "There are *two* dogs."

Another stretch of silence filled the media room.

Finally, the TV switched to the gameshow and someone, Randy wasn't sure who, muted it. On the screen, it appeared most of the audience voted for Bram as their first hunter.

All of that didn't really matter right now.

"We have two dogs in the same town," Randy said.

"And hunters going in to kill Lon," Micheal Jules said.

"It looked feral," Edward Mosk said.

"I believe it was," Randy said. "No other dogs have escaped."

"You sure?" Doug spouted.

Randy rolled his eyes. "Yes. I'm fucking sure."

"Maybe we should cancel," Jeff said.

Randy stood and swayed a bit from the booze. "No." He pointed at the TV. "We don't cancel. We don't tell anyone." He grinned. "This about to get more interesting."

Randy refilled his glass with scotch and sat down just as the hunters were being dropped off on the outskirts of Dyer.

CHAPTER 15

LON WALKED THE night, stomach groaning. The dog part was hungry and needed food to keep its metabolism sated. But the human part was at the forefront now and deep in thought. There was another dog in town. Something feral.

He ventured into the woods and thought about running. Just use the dog part and run as far away from the town as he could. He was done fighting. Retired. If the other dog wanted the town, then it could have it.

Before he could delve into the idea of running more, the dog part shoved him back out of starvation.

The dog part of Lon shivered, snorted and glanced around. Food was the only thing on his mind. He needed food and he needed it now. He drew in the air, searching for a scent. Any scent. At this point he would eat a damn boot. He was about to move away from the woods and go back to town when a tasty scent caught his attention. He spun and sprinted toward the scent.

A deep growl gurgled in his throat. Already he felt his strength waning.

He crashed through brambles and thicket and stumbled directly into a big bald man. His eyes widened and he stumbled away while struggling to put his night goggles on. A large gun was slung over his shoulder.

Lon, starving, lunged at the big man. The big man smacked Lon away as he secured the night vision goggles over his eyes. Lon huffed. No human had ever done that to him before.

The big man lifted his giant gun and pointed it at Lon.

Lon yelped and leaped away before the gun boomed. He rolled through the weeds and sprang up, ready to attack but the big man swung an axe and buried it into Lon's left shoulder. Lon yelped in pain. He glanced at the big man in time to see the big gun being pointed at him.

He sprang to the side, though not fast enough. The slug struck his right leg and he went spiraling into the woods. Pain exploded up his leg to his hip. He rolled around in the weeds, howling in agony. He thought he saw something floating next to a nearby tree before it dipped out of sight. He was in too much pain to care.

"Didn't see this shit comin'," the big man said as he picked Lon up, "Did ya?" He threw Lon out of the woods.

Lon rolled from side to side. Pain laced his body. From the axe wound to the leg wound. He couldn't think and the big man was reloading his big gun now.

Move, the human part screamed at him. *Move or he'll kill us!*

Lon gritted his teeth and scrambled away from the big man.

"Ah, don't be scared," the big man shouted and barked laughter. "I just wanna pet ya!"

Run, the human part of Lon cried.

But he couldn't run. Not with his wounded leg. It hurt too much. There was only one option.

Lon spun, dashed to the right. The gun exploded the night, slug missing him this time. Using his good leg, he sprang at the big man before the man had time to grab his axe. Lon slammed the big man to the ground, knocking the wind out of him. The big man tried to grab at Lon, but he dodged the hands and countered by slashing his claws across the man's face. One of Lon's claws snagged on the right eye, slicing through it. The eyeball oozed out of its socket.

As hungry as Lon was, he licked up the gelatinous eyeball while the big man wailed and thrashed in pain.

The taste of the eyeball reignited Lon's ravenous hunger. He reared and lunged, sinking his teeth into the big man's face. He thrashed back and forth, ripping through flesh and crunching bone. Lon tore the big man's face off, along with a portion of his skull, and chomped it all down. The food spurred desperation and Lon cracked open the rest of the

big man's skull and ate the brains, the bits of bone.
He couldn't stop. He needed food.

Lon ate almost every bit of the big man.

THE DOG FOUNDATION

RANDY DROPPED HIS glass of scotch the moment Lon tore Bram's face off.

He wasn't expecting that. Bram looked like he was about to win everything there for a few minutes but…

He had to look away when Lon began eating the man.

"Oh, shit," Doug Tremp said.

"Can't they cut to a commercial or something?" Micheal said.

"Oh, my," Rodney Quinn shouted as the show switched abruptly to the studio. Rodney flashed his bright smile at the camera. "That was something, wasn't it?" He swept across the stage and gestured at the audience which had fallen silent.

Rodney sighed and lowered his head a bit. In a lower tone, he said, "I know what you're all thinking." He sat on the edge of the stage and looked out at the audience.

Randy, who was creeping into drunk territory a few minutes ago sat straight in his chair, not feeling the affects of the booze at all. *It's over*, he thought. *That was too much for people.*

"You thought this would be a fun game without any violence." Rodney nodded. "I know." He gradually swept his gaze back and forth across the sea of people. "But we here at the Dog Foundation will only show the truth." He smiled a bit. "And the truth is that Lon Crandel, that slobbering dog..." He stood. "...that mindless werewolf! That evil eating machine! He's dangerous and the bad guy. If you didn't know that before..." Rodney paused for effect. "Now you do."

Randy snorted. "Damn, he's good."

The others concurred.

Making Lon the real monster, the bad guy, was genius. It was something Randy hoped the audience would come up with on their own, but Rodney slamming the point home was fantastic.

Rodney walked from one end of the stage to the other. "Our hearts go out to Big Bram. He was a good family man. A father. He loved hunting."

"Is any of that real?" Jeff asked.

Randy smirked. "Only the hunting part. Bram had no immediate family."

"He died doing what he loved, and we will compensate his family handsomely for it." Rodney beamed a smile at the audience. "What do you think? Should the show go on? Should we save Dyer from this ravenous dog?"

The audience was silent as the cameras panned over them. Then, all at once, they cheered. So loud even Rodney covered his ears. A literal explosion of cheers.

"Big Bram is gone! Vote for your next hero!"

Randy sat back in his chair smiling. The show was a hit.

Thank god.

CHAPTER 16

Lon CHEWED THE meat off one of the big man's femurs and walked toward his shed. Best to get back to the safety of the shed for now. He would need to eat again before dawn, but for now... he was sated.

With all the food, Lon's injuries were almost healed already. Still sore as hell and it hurt to walk on the injured leg, but ten times better than before eating the big man. Sometimes being a dog was okay. If you ate enough food, the body would heal itself. The night was renewed, but...

What was the big man doing here? The human part spoke up in his head.

The dog part shook his head. He didn't know, nor really care.

I think he was using an elephant gun, the human part said. *And what was with the axe?*

The dog part hated it when the human part tried

to talk to him. But he guessed the human made a good point. Why was the big man there? Why did he have a… well whatever the human part called it. A big ass gun.

He bit down, crunching through the femur and sucked out the marrow. Then he ate the rest of the bone. The frog and crickets did their noisy thing. Bats swept through the air catching bugs. Other than the memory of the big man trying to kill him, it was a perfect night.

Something is wrong, the human part said, and the dog part rolled his eyes. So much for a perfect night. *The other dog. The big man with the big gun…*

Lon huffed and shook his vulpine head. He hadn't thought about the other dog. The one that tore a woman and her kids apart. The one that pissed all over their corpses. Marked its territory. A feral thing to do. Lon couldn't remember a time he marked his territory or area. After his tenth fight he almost pissed on a mutilated dog as an act of superiority, but Master stopped him. Master trained him well and…

A strange scent drifted by him. He flared his nostrils, inhaling as much of the scent as he could. It wasn't the other dog. It was pleasant. He turned in the direction of the lovely aroma. Then, just as quickly as he caught the scent, he lost it. He snorted and frowned. A low growl rumbled in his throat. He moved around, sniffing and tasting the air. He listened for any odd sound.

Despite all of that, he couldn't find the scent again and the town had fallen into a slumber. There was one thing that snagged his attention, though.

The crickets and frogs were silent. Lon scanned his surroundings. He stood in someone's large backyard. The house itself stood at least fifty feet away. There was a garden shed not too far from him. An old, massive oak tree with its thick, twisted branches took over most of the yard closest him.

Something wasn't right. A tingly sensation of someone… or something watching sent shivers through him and made the hackles on the back of his neck stiffened. His gaze lifted to the old oak tree. He stared at the branches. He watched the leaves shift in a slight breeze for a while.

Eventually he looked away from the tree and a bit of dust or something tickled his right nostril into a sneeze. He shook his head and turned in a full circle, trying to catch any movements or sounds or scents. Anything.

But there was nothing.

He moved out of the yard but chose not to return to the shed. Someone or something was hunting him. Maybe the breeze would shift in the right direction, and he would be able to pinpoint where his hunter was. Until then, Lon intended to remain vigilant.

THE DOG FOUNDATION

"HE DOESN'T KNOW she's there," Rodney whispered. "Who is our hunter? Our hero?" He smiled his bright smile while. On the screen behind him a short, blond woman wielding a crossbow. "Yes…" Rodney crooned for the audience then the camera.

Fireworks exploded on either side of the stage and Rodney Quinn lifted his arms. The display was captivating.

"Yes!" More fireworks erupted. "It's our crossbow wielding Kelly! Place your votes! Will it be Kelly to put the beast down or one of our other three heroes? Place your votes now!"

Rodney walked back and forth on stage with Kelly posing on the screen behind him. The ticking clock sound echoed throughout the studio while the audience entered their votes.

The timer dinged and Rodney chuckled into the microphone. "This was a quick vote." He smiled at the audience. "And the results are in!" He checked a small device in his hand and stuffed it back into the inside pocket of his suit jacket.

"Y'all," Rodney said. "It's almost unanimous." He grinned. "Isn't that somethin'?" He paused and smiled for a few seconds. Finally, he walked to center stage. "Are you ready to see who our new hero is?"

The audience roared. A sound so loud people in the town five miles away heard it.

Once they fell silent, Rodney nodded and cocked a thumb over his shoulder at the screen. "Our new hero, ladies and gentlemen, is…" Sam popped up on the screen, twirling his revolvers like an old western star. Sam, with his high and tight hair cut and red handlebar mustache. "Sam!" Rodney spun and pointed at the screen. "Let's see what's happening now!"

CHAPTER 17

LON DECIDED TO move toward the woods again.

He was being followed… hunted. Either it was human or the other dog, but he was almost certain it wasn't the other dog. He would smell its strong stench. But maybe it was another dog. An older, better hunter.

Didn't matter. Lon hated the feeling of something hunting him and he couldn't find it. Whatever it was, maybe—

"Hey, dog," a man said in a deep, heavily southern accent.

Lon stopped, huffed and glanced around. At first, he didn't see the man standing next to the large pine tree. There was no scent. Maybe the pine sap covered it? Lon didn't know. There was no time to think too much.

The man wasn't as big or tall as the Big Man, but

there was something different in his eyes. Something… more predatory. A strange mix of intelligence and insanity. A man who was unpredictable.

"Ya got five seconds t'run," the man with the revolvers said. "One…"

Lon frowned at the revolvers. His human side told him there were only twelve bullets between the two guns. Which meant, if Lon could dodge those bullets the man would be open for an attack when he tried to reload.

A deep growl bubbled in his throat and the man with the mustache grunted. "Champion dog, my ass."

Anger sparked inside Lon, igniting rage. He hated the man. He hated the way the man's voice sounded. He hated the way the man grinned. He hated the man's chuckle.

The man with the mustache snorted and spat. He frowned at Lon. "Ya challengin' me, boy? That what you're doin'?" He laughed, shook his head, and thumbed the hammers back on the revolvers. "Well, alright, my furry friend." His face hardened. "Let's dance."

Lon's eyes narrowed. He dropped to all fours and began to circle the man. Waiting.

"Yeah," the man with the mustache said. "Ya'think you're tough?"

Lon growled.

The man grinned. "Ya don't got the guts."

Lon grinned in response, revealing his long, sharp teeth. The man acted like it didn't bother him, but Lon caught a hint of fear flop across his white, freckled face. The man liked to act tough, but deep down…

The man's right shoulder twitched, and Lon dashed to the side before the man could pull the trigger. He pounced at the man, but the man was a lot quicker than the big man from earlier and dodged Lon's attack.

"Woo," the man shouted. "You're a spunky one, ain't ya?" He pointed a revolver at Lon. "Betcha can't beat a bullet."

He fired before Lon could move. Searing pain drilled into his right shoulder. He stumbled a bit, glanced at the smoking hole in his shoulder. A deep growl rumbled in his throat and glared at the man with the mustache. The man's Adam's apple bobbed. He pointed his revolver.

Lon sprang to the right a second before the man squeezed the trigger. The shot went wild, and Lon pounced on top of the man. He clawed through the man's right hand, leaving the hand in bloody ribbons and knocked the revolver into darkness. Lon smacked the other revolver away just as it went off. The thunderous noise made Lon's ears ring. He shook his head and lunged for the man's face.

A sharp pain struck the middle of his back. He yelped and scrambled off the man with mustache and glanced around. He reached around and found a stick, or something embedded in his back. Where did it even come from? It hurt like hell, but he didn't have time to dwell on it because the man with the mustache was getting to his feet.

"Ya motherfucker," the man said and held up what was left of his right hand. "Look what ya fuckin' did!" He pulled a large knife from its sheath attached to his hip near the left holster and pointed it at Lon. "Now ya fuckin' die!"

Lon was about to attack when a sharp pain struck the back of his left leg and he dropped to his knees.

The man with the mustache grunted. "Pulled a damn hammy, didn't ya." He chuckled as he strolled closer to Lon. He swung the big knife back and forth like a wagging finger. "Always remember to stretch before goin' on murderous rampages, boy."

Lon growled. His gaze drifted from the knife to the shoulder and fixed on the man's sweaty face for a few seconds before drifting to the shoulder again. There was someone else out there shooting him with things, but he needed to take care of the man first. But just as he was about to, another sharp pain stung his right shoulder. Waiting for a twitch.

The man stopped, frowned, and glared into the night behind Lon. He glowered for a second or two and thrust the knife into Lon's chest.

"He's mine," the man shouted. "He's mine!"

Lon roared, gripped the man by the throat and stood on his hind legs. The man gargled, gasping for air while his suspended legs kicked at Lon. It hurt to stand like that with the leg and back wounds, but enough was enough. Already the pain was subsiding and his body pushing what the human part said now might be arrows out of his body.

As for the knife currently stuck in his chest… ?

The blade didn't go deep enough to do any real damage.

His claw sank into the man's neck. The man

lashed, gurgling and not finding air. Blood streamed over Lon's claw and soaked into his fur. Lon shivered the second the man's blood slithered into his nostrils. So sweet. So delicious.

Lon yanked the man forward, ripping most of the man's throat out. He ate the man's larynx, skin, muscle, tendons and a bit of spine. He dropped the man's twitching body and tore into the abdomen, where most of the nutrients were. He slurped the gallbladder down and tore the liver out. He was almost finished with the liver when that strange, sweet scent caught his attention again.

Not the other dog. But whoever was hunting him.

He dropped the remaining liver and turned around to find a small woman, only about half the height of the man with the mustache.

She cocked her head to the side and grinned. In her hands she held a loaded crossbow aimed directly at him. "Looking for me?" She fired an arrow into his left shoulder.

He yelped. That one hurt worse than the others. Maybe because she was closer?

The woman's crossbow was equipped with a drum that rotated, feeding a new arrow into the crossbow.

She chuckled. "Does it hurt?" She aimed the crossbow at the Lon's head. "I've been waiting a long time to take one of you out." She stepped a little closer. "My mother says hello."

Lon's eyes widened and he leaped to the side, dodging the arrow.

He ripped the arrow out of his left shoulder and

the back of his right shoulder. When he glanced at the woman, she wasn't there.

Lon gritted his teeth. He was tired of the games and couldn't wait to crack her skull open and feast on the gray wrinkles of her brain.

If he could catch her.

He sniffed, trying to catch her scent, but try as he might… it was like she never existed.

Lon growled and slowly investigated his surroundings. She could be anywhere. The woman knew how to stay upwind and quiet enough he couldn't hear. He wasn't about to turn his back on her either. The arrows hurt but didn't go deep enough to do any real damage before he began healing again.

Still, if she was able sneak up close enough behind him and shoot an arrow through the back of his head…

He turned in a full circle. Once there was no trace of the woman, he moved on all fours to where she was standing. He caught her scent on the grass and followed it to a nearby tree. That's where the scent ended. He sniffed the tree to see if maybe she climbed up it to hide, but her scent wasn't there.

We need to get out of here, the human part of him said. *There are people hunting us.*

Lon growled, slowly scanning the area once more. The woman was out there somewhere, and he didn't want to leave without ripping her heart out. So, instead of listening to the human part, he crawled around searching for the woman. She was close, he knew it. He felt it. There was no way she could run far away without him noticing. He would hear her running.

No, she was hiding incredibly well. But where… ?

After a while of searching, he gave up. There simply was no trace of her. He ate some more of the man with the mustache and moved away from the area. The woman with the crossbow had some kind of vendetta against dogs like him. The rage in her eyes… the way she nearly spat her words at him…

He walked on all fours so he wouldn't be so noticeable. There were people hunting him and he didn't know why.

It's the people who pay the Old Man, the human part said. *They're hunting us because we escaped.*

It took Lon a bit to figure out who the Old Man was. Master.

He stopped and turned in a slow circle, but there weren't any new scents or sounds. He walked away from the town. His stomach was heavy for now, but he knew the hunger would grip him before dawn.

Right now, however, he just wanted to get away from everything. All the noises of town and all the conflicting scents.

He just needed to get some peace.

Just a bit of time to—

He heard the odd thumping a second before a woman, not the crossbow woman, said, "Hey, dog!" She giggled. "Ready to die?"

THE DOG FOUNDATION

Randy, now too drunk to move, chuckled and pointed at the screen while Rodney Quinn blasted Lon Crandel. The others glanced at him but were more interested in the show.

Rodney paced the stage. "Ladies and gentlemen... we lost another good soul. Sam was his name. A lovely man. A good Christian. A peacekeeper and fantastic hunter." He sighed heavily into the mic. "His family will be compensated for his bravery."

The audience was silent. More than a few were weeping over a man they never knew.

Rodney lifted his head and glanced over the audience, not lingering on a single face in the sea of ten thousand people. His frown gradually grew into a smile.

"But we *still* have three hunters, three *heroes*."

Behind him the three remaining hunters popped up on the screen. "Left to right. Kelly!" A scattering of applause. "We saw her deadly crossbow action just a little while ago! There's Will! Our favorite sniper, just waiting for the right moment. And here's Em! Always ready to rock!"

The audience applauded, though not with the gusto earlier in the show. Some people appeared disgusted. Frowning, the corners of their mouths turned down. Others appeared to be ill or on the verge of puking all over.

Rodney, realizing he was losing the audience, amped it up a little. He pointed at the remaining hunters, cuing intense music.

"Our heroes, ladies and gentlemen! Our heroes! Which one will take down the dog? Which one will save the town! Which one will make you rich?"

He paused, smiling into the lights so that his teeth glimmered like diamonds.

"Save the town," he shouted. "Save the children!"

This roused the audience. Their applause erupted in thunderous fashion. Rodney beamed. With the audience revitalized, Rodney calmed them down. He grinned.

"Now," he said. "We have a special surprise for you." He nodded and the lights dimmed a bit. Low, deep drumbeats rose gradually. "Shh…" Rodney moved to the far right of the stage. "Are you ready?" The drumbeats grew in volume for a few seconds then died out.

Rodney, still on the far right, lighting still dim, nodded. "Yes…" The stage erupted in fireworks.

The audience screamed and howled. "Let me introduce you all to our new hunter," Rodney shouted. "Our new hero!"

A large man stepped onto the stage. His arms were chained, and his right ankle was tethered by another thick chain attached to something out of sight.

The audience fell silent as the man stood and stared blankly out at them. He dominated the stage with his presence. His glistening bare chest. His massive muscles.

In the viewing room, Randy sat up. Even in his drunken stupor, he realized something was off. "That a damn dog?"

No one answered him.

Eventually he sat back. Another dog wasn't part of the deal. He shook his head, and the room began to spin.

"Fuck," he managed before vomiting all over himself.

Rodney chuckled as he crossed the stage to the large, chained man. He patted the man's shoulder. "We found this dog in Dyer. You know, the same town our heroes are hunting Lon Crandel." Rodney pointed at the large man. "This dog is so feral; he has no name." The audience gasped. "But we'll call him Bob."

The audience booed a bit, but Rodney smiled and waved them off.

"I know, I know," Rodney said and paced back and forth on the stage while the large man followed his movement with his eyes. "He's a dog and we're hunting a dog. But!" He paused for a bit. "But!" He patted the big man's shoulder again and the man glared at him. Rodney, noticing the glare, moved quickly away. "But, but… but!"

Rodney chuckled and gestured at the large man on stage. "This feral dog will be on a short leash! Yes! The shortest, I assure you." He smiled. "He is our attack dog and will be controlled by our remaining heroes." He paused while the audience took it all in. "And once his usefulness is over…" Rodney nodded and pointed at the other man on stage. "He will be put down and the threat eliminated."

The man turned his head and glowered at Rodney.

Rodney didn't notice, but the cameras caught the twist of anger on the man's grimy face.

The audience, however, was focused on Rodney as he pointed at the screen. The studio went dark.

"Now," Rodney said. "Let's see what Lon Crandel is up to."

The screen flickered and focused on Lon running through the woods.

CHAPTER 18

Lon, RACING THROUGH the woods on all fours, chased a nice, juicy doe. It was like clockwork. The night was almost over and the hunger was all he cared about. Those hunting him didn't matter.

He thought he heard the *wup-wup-wup* of a helicopter, but that didn't matter either.

Nor did the strange black things zipping around him while he ran. The human part called them drones.

Didn't matter.

What mattered was ripping the deer's throat out and lapping up her hot blood. What mattered was the ropey flesh and tender entrails. What mattered was sustenance and the energy that would follow.

He leaped over a fallen tree, crashed through brambles, and skidded to the right as the doe tried to shoot around a tree and trick him. Instead of following her, he sprinted around the tree, catching her before she could dart away. She cried out a second before he buried his teeth into her throat. He wrestled her to the ground, claws deep in her sides. Blood filled his mouth and he tried to swallow it all down as it spurted, but there was just too much at once.

It didn't take long. The doe stopped struggling and Lon ripped her throat out. He chewed through the sinews, tendons, and juicy muscle and swallowed it all down. Fur and all. The fur didn't bother him one bit.

He moved to her midsection, tearing through her hide and spilling her entrails all over the weedy ground. The aroma made all his insides clench with hunger. He might as well be a man stranded on a desert island seeing a steak for the first time in weeks. Lon dove into his prey and feasted until he was full.

Stomach, distended with a majority of the doe, Lon staggered deeper into the woods. Maybe he could just hide out here until dawn from the people hunting him. They wouldn't come for him in the woods… would they?

His bulging stomach gurgled. He could lie down right now and sleep, though he knew his metabolism would kick in soon and he'd be running. Hell, maybe he could even hunt his hunters before dawn hit.

The drones zipped around him. One followed slowly behind him. His human part told him to smash them, but right now Lon didn't even feel like moving. He walked a bit farther and leaned against a tree for a bit. The whines of the drones were getting to him, though. He glared at one hovering nearby. It floated a few inches closer, and he growled. The camera at the center of the thing extended a bit.

He smacked the damn thing so hard it crashed into the tree next to him. It twitched on the ground, trying to fly, but one of its propellers was broken. It spun and sputtered on the ground like a dying insect.

Lon growled and stomped on the drone until was nothing but broken plastic. He snorted and glanced at the others hovering around him. They all flinched and zipped away.

They'll be back, the human part said. *Need to find a place to hide*.

Lon huffed and looked around. Hide? No, that's not what he was going to do. He couldn't do that.

His stomach grumbled and trembled as his metabolism kicked in. He lurched, fire burning throughout his body.

He dropped to his knees, reared back, and howled. The night seemed to pause just for him. The crickets and frogs stopped. The other wildlife paused. A nearby raccoon sniffed the air, shivered and waddled quickly away in the opposite direction.

His howl faded and he slumped in the middle of the woods for a minute. His back heaved with every breath, spine popping like bubble wrap. A rush of heat flooded through his veins and the pain eased. He huffed, blinked and glanced around. His heart thrummed and all he wanted to do was run but...

A slim silhouette cartwheeled from behind one

tree to another. His eyes narrowed. His nostrils flared, catching her scent. Yes. A female. But not the one with the crossbow. This one had a strong odor. Not from sweat and bacteria. Well, not all of it. There was an underlying smell. Something... evil. Something mean. Her essence screamed insanity. Just by drawing in her scent, he knew she enjoyed what she did.

Unlike the other female, however, she wasn't good at keeping still and staying upwind. On her scent alone, he could pinpoint which tree she was behind and which one she moved to. Always moving, this one. He growled and bared his teeth. His desire, no, *urge* to run was now funneled into ripping and tearing. The need for blood. Carnage.

He followed the sounds of her movements and scent from tree to tree as she circled him.

He was about to attack when her movements stopped, and he lost her scent. Lon froze, frowned. She was trickier than he first thought. His human part told him to be careful. He told Lon that the female was laying a trap. He said, "She's different than the others."

Lon's growl rose in volume as he turned slowly in a circle. He stood in a small clearing, and she could be hiding behind any of the larger trees. It was an old forest, so most of the trees were large. He could feel the forest's age like a small ache in his back. He was linked to it in some way he could not understand. It was old. Very old. And it watched Lon with a weariness so deep he felt it quiver under his paws.

He waited for her to move. He waited for that

movement to also give away both her position and scent. But she didn't move. She remained behind one of the trees surrounding him. But which one? Lon turned in a slow circle, hoping to catch a whiff of her scent. No such luck.

Gradually, the night awakened again. First the crickets and frogs. Then some fireflies winked into existence and floated above the weeds and tall grasses of the small clearing he stood in. An owl hooted somewhere deeper in the woods. Then…

"You're gonna die," the woman teased. Her giggles bounced off every tree, disorientating him for a bit.

Lon paced slowly back and forth, trying to look everywhere at once. His heart bashed against his ribs. She was out there. She was close.

A shiver trickled through him. Which tree was she behind? Which one… ?

He crept closer to one of the trees and stopped. The air tasted damp and sweet with the nightly dew. Somewhere, probably in town, someone screamed. Sounded like a man this time. Lon's mind flickered to the other dog. The feral one that tore a woman and her children to meaty, red ribbons.

A stick snapped, drawing his attention back to the woman hiding behind one of the trees.

He started forward again and stopped.

Something was wrong. A trap? Yes. It smelled like a trap. She wanted him to come to her. He backed away from the tree toward the center of the clearing. The human part of him was frustratingly silent now. In a time when Lon needed the bastard the most, of course, he fell asleep or whatever the asshole was doing instead of helping.

It was a stalemate.

He could charge and attack every tree. But then he left himself unaware and vulnerable if she snuck up behind him. So… it was a waiting game. Something his jumpy nerves screamed in dismay. His body thrummed with energy that needed to be burned off before dawn. He didn't know why, just that he needed to do it, or bad things would happen. Maybe it was something Master taught him, though he couldn't fully remember.

Lon's gaze drifted from tree to tree as he turned in a slow, calculated circle.

Minutes rolled by and what felt like hours. His nerves, his entire body cried for him to do something. They pleaded. He needed to release the energy before—

He caught the faintest glimpse of movement in his right peripheral,

Lon swung around and caught a bullet in the chest. He staggered back a half step, teeth gritted against the pain. Blood dampened his fur and trickled down his torso.

The woman lowered her gun. A small one. A—

That's an uzi, the human part of him said. *She has two. They shoot really fast.*

Oh, *now* the bastard spoke up. Because of course. Better late than never, Lon supposed.

Small bullets, the human part said. *But really fast and a lot of them.*

Lon huffed out a harsh breath and growled at the woman.

"Gotcha," she said, smiled and shined a light on

him.

She wore black lipstick, and her dark hair was pulled back in a tight ponytail. Her eyes were wide… insane. She stared directly at him and grinned. For the longest time, she stood there pointing an uzi at him and grinning.

Every muscle in Lon told him to take her out, but his mind and the human part told him to wait. The woman was too hyper focused on him.

"Lot of people watchin'ya right now, doggie," the woman said and snickered. "Millions of people."

Lon growled and the woman giggled, as though in pleasure.

"Yep," she said. "You're on a game show, hon. Your head has a high price tag!"

He didn't know what the hell she was talking about. All he knew was he wanted to split her open and feast on her insides.

The woman cocked her head to the side, still grinning. "Should we give'em a show?"

Lon lowered his head a bit, eyes narrowing.

"Ohhh," she said and giggled. "Look at you, big doggie."

Lon moved to the left a bit and she followed his movement with her uzi.

"I gotcha, big doggie." She skipped closer, her gun always fixed on him while the other uzi in her left hand swung back and forth with her arm like a pendulum. She stopped a few feet away and pointed both uzis at him. "Bang-bang!"

Lon darted to the side a split second before she pulled the triggers. Both guns spat bullets as he swung to her left, dipped, and slashed her upper right thigh with his claws. She shrieked, spinning around, fingers still holding the triggers. Lon ducked and lunged at her again, still catching a few bullets in his shoulder. He ignored the pain and focused on killing her.

She flipped backward a few feet. He almost pounced, but she was too quick. Even before the flip was complete, she had the uzis trained on him. Her wild scent obliterated his thoughts for a minute. He wanted to kill her. He wanted to eat her. He wanted it done.

He just needed a way to do so with minimal damage to himself.

Then again... the more he ate the faster he healed. Could he die from too many bullets? Master never told him, and the human part didn't know. What if he didn't eat something after taking all those bullets? Would he die then?

"I'll take my money now," the woman said and squeezed the triggers.

The first spatter of bullets struck his shoulders. Lon yelped, dipped and shot at the woman with a roar. She flipped out of the way. Pain lashed across his back as she buried bullets into it. He staggered, swung a claw at her and missed. She laughed, sank into the splits and shot littered his chest with bloody holes.

Lon whined and glanced around. The pain was bad. Really bad. Worse than any pain he'd felt before. So many bullets. Too many. He slumped and shuffled toward the woman, meaning to claw her face off, but she giggled and cartwheeled away.

"You're gonna die, big doggie."

He was healing. He felt it. But it was slow. Far too slow. He shivered, trying to focus on the woman rather than the pain but the task was beyond him. She danced around him, laughing and spraying him with more bullets. Lon coughed up blood and dropped to his knees.

He was going to die. There was no question now. After everything, all the blood drenched fights and illnesses, a woman with uzis would be his end. The pain created a gray cloud in his mind. His thoughts were sluggish. His strength waned. Yes, he was healing but there were too many bullets in him. Too much damage. It was taking too long to heal.

The woman pressed the tiny muzzle of an uzi against the side of his head.

"Any last growls?"

A massive shiver racked Lon and he whined from the agony.

She laughed and leaned in close. "Remember to smile for the cameras, doggie."

She backed away and a sharp spike of agony slammed into his chest. Just above the heart. He yelped and leaned forward a bit. Blood mixed with saliva dangled in scarlet strings from his open mouth. His muzzle quivered.

"No," the woman with the uzi shouted. "You can't have him! He's *mine*!"

"Oh, shut the fuck up, you idiot." It didn't take long for Lon to recognize the voice of the woman with the crossbow. "We get equal shares."

"I don't care, Kelly," the woman with the uzis said. "I got'im, dead-bang. He's mine."

"I got a score to settle," Kelly said. Her tone was low, nearly a growl.

"So?" The woman with uzis said. "I'm about to end this so we can—"

"Shut up, Em," Kelly said. "Get out of the way so I can end it. I've waited a long time for this."

Slowly, Em's bullets seeped out of the wounds and tumbled to the ground. The wounds themselves closed. Kelly's arrow was too fresh yet to move. Regardless... he was healing. While they bickered, he was regaining his strength. He drew in a shuddery breath and blew it out slowly while his insides healed.

"I'm not moving," Em said and stood in front of Lon. Her back to him.

"My god," Kelly said. "You truly are an idiot, aren't you..." It wasn't a question.

"Don't call me an idiot, *bitch*."

"Listen, you little—"

A distant howl rose above their bickering and silence them. They both turned in the direction of the howl.

Lon's heart thudded heavily. That wasn't a friendly howl. It wasn't saying hello. No... that was a hungry howl. A feral howl.

Lon gritted his teeth as he quietly slipped away from the two women. He needed to get upwind and find a place to hide. He leapt, kicked off a nearby tree to another. He needed to get his scent off the ground and buy him some time. He was about to move upwind when the other dog roared. A deep, guttural sound struck a deep nerve in Lon. He stumbled, lost his balance and dropped to the ground and skidded into a tangle of thick brambles.

He crawled through the twists of thorns until they thinned out and rested for a few seconds. His body was still in the throes of healing and moving was still a bit rough.

Both women had fallen utterly silent. If Kelly, the woman with the crossbow, was smart, she would find a good hiding spot upwind before—

"Holy shit," Em shouted. "Nobody told me about a second dog!"

"Because there wasn't supposed to be two, dumbass."

A few ticks of silence followed.

Lon drew in a whiff of a rogue breeze. Yes. There. Just barely. A hint of something foul. The reek of feral musk. The other dog was close. Very close. It knew they were here and closing in silently. Lon was about as upwind as he could get for now until he knew the other dog's position. He crouched behind a large tree and peeked around it until he spotted the two women.

Kelly knew how to hunt. She fooled Lon and she could probably fool the other dog. But she wasn't moving. Why? Why not use the same tactics to confuse the dog?

Lon's gaze floated away from the women and scanned the forest beyond as far as he could see back and forth. So far, there was no visual sign of the feral dog. He waited. He watched. But the feral dog didn't show. If it was out there, it would be hiding and waiting. Waiting for what? Lon didn't know. He would have attacked right away. Slaughtered both women if he was at full strength.

Eventually, both women hurried away, and Lon made his way toward his shed. Dawn was closing in and he wanted to be hidden in the shed when the human part took over.

He just hoped he'd make it before sunrise.

CHAPTER 19

THE SCENT OF the shed was close.

Lon ate a raccoon along the way to speed up the healing. Soon enough, Kelly's arrow was shoved out of his chest and fell to the ground. He barely noticed. All he wanted was to get to the shed and rest. As far as he knew, none of those little drones were following him. At least he hoped so. Likewise, the feral dog. Which, if it was like him, would also be seeking some kind of shelter to rest in.

The first few birds chirped. The air around him began taking on a golden hue. Dawn was about to arrive. Sunrise now would mean he'd be left exposed in the woods.

Lon dashed into a sprint for the shed. Racing the daylight as the first sheen of the sun peeked over the horizon. Weariness swelled in him like a water balloon. His sprint slowed to a run. His breathing turned ragged and wheezy. He burst through a thicket and onto the property where his shed stood. He glanced at the barn, which was closer, but it was the shed he wanted to be. The barn was too open and anyone walking by could see him in there.

The sun rose a bit more over the trees, spilling golden light over him and the town.

He stumbled and fell to his knees. A low whine escaped him as he crawled to the shed. The sun rose higher just as Lon opened the shed door and dragged himself inside, his lower body already changing into the human part. Furless human legs kicked sluggishly trying to close the shed's door. Lon wanted to lock the door, but the best he could do was lie against it. A violent shiver shot through him. A bright white light and…

Lon blinked, gagged and crawled away from the door as the rest of the dog part of him went to sleep. He wrapped one of the blankets he stole around him, teeth chattering from the chill consuming him. It wasn't always like this. Changing from the dog to his human self, but sometimes it was and other times it would be worse.

He chalked it up to all the stress through the night. Stress that made him unusually tired after waking up. Normally, he would be fully awake and ready to function. But right now… all he wanted to do was wrap up like a burrito and take a long nap. Yes. That's exactly what he needed.

Lon locked the shed's door, found a nice spot out of sight, curled up in the blanket with another blanket under his head as pillow and drifted off to sleep.

CHAPTER 20

HE WOKE TO the sound of children laughing.

Lon sucked in a sharp breath and wrestled with the blanket he was curled up in, heart stammering. He rolled onto the center of the shed's floor, body slick with sweat. It was hot and he regretted the blanket he had slept in. He drank some warm water from the jug, armed sweat from his face, and glanced around.

The shed door was still locked. Everything seemed fine and he was questioning if he really heard children laughing or if it was just a—

"That's raccoon shit," a kid shouted. "My dad showed me what it looks like."

"The house is haunted," another kid said. "My grandpa said two people were murdered in there by a hobo."

Lon got dressed in jeans and a t-shirt, slipped on

the pair of boots and tried to peek out the window but it was too slathered in age old grime to see through.

"Guys," one of the kids shouted. "Check out the barn!"

"If Mom knew I was here she'd be pissed."

"The barn is lame, bro."

"Maybe we should go back," this one sounded like a girl. "Dad said there might be a rabid bear around here."

They talked amongst themselves, but all Lon heard were mumbles through the wooden walls of the shed.

He drank more warm water and ate a slice of bread. He listened, but if the children were out there, he couldn't hear them.

He waited. For what felt like hours… he waited and drank more water.

Eventually, he opened the shed's door. It creaked on its rusty hinges, and he cringed. Any second now one of the kids would shout, "There's someone in the shed!" and his cover would be blown. His hideout would be compromised, and he would have to find a different one or run. And he didn't want to run right now. He wanted the town to be his forever home.

But after everything… and knowing he was a part of some deranged gameshow…

Lon stepped out of the shed. He stood there, just beyond the threshold, and waited a few minutes. There were no signs of the children. So, either they were in the barn, or they left the property. Either way, he still should be able to hear them. He frowned and stared at the barn. The big doors weren't open. It was as if the kids disappeared into thin air.

He backed up into the shed, found an old rusty sickle and peeked through the open doorway again. Something was wrong. It was too quiet. Not even the birds were singing.

Yes, something was wrong. Maybe the people hunting him found him? Maybe they tracked him to the shed? The dog part had been struggling and his mind on survival rather than being aware of a drone or something following him.

"Shit," Lon said and glanced around. So far, however, he didn't spot anything out of the ordinary.

Nearby, a bird began to sing. A few others joined in. After a few more minutes, the world outside the shed came back to life.

But what made them go silent in the first place? The kids?

Lon, still clutching the sickle, emerged from the shed and walked around the property. There was no sign of the kids, other than a Snicker's candy bar wrapper near the hydrant. He drank from the hydrant and continued checking out the property. The kids weren't in the barn or anywhere.

Maybe they rode to his place on bikes? Maybe that's how they slipped away so quickly...

He stood near the road and frowned at the town in the distance. Eventually, he saw four figures on what could be bicycles near the outskirts of town.

Lon sighed relief while grasshoppers flicked through the tall weeds he stood in. He blinked and glanced around. He needed to get out of sight before the gameshow he was in found him. That was if they didn't already know where he was. He thought that they might and were giving him a break. It was no fun hunting a human after all...

He returned to the shed, opened a can of soup and ate it all cold. He thought about taking a nap but decided to build an alarm system on the shed's door instead using the empty cans of food. In the rafters he found a few partial sheets of particle board and a couple dust laden two by fours. There were a few nails and he used them to fix a piece of the particle board over the window. The two by fours he used to create a barricade of sorts across the center of the door. Something strong enough to give him some time to wake up and fight before someone broke in.

Once his nerves settled a bit, Lon ventured outside again. He stood near the edge of the property, fairly certain he wasn't being watched, and thought about going to town. He needed to know what they were saying down there. He needed more information. If he could move through town unnoticed maybe he could eavesdrop enough to gather some form of intel. Maybe he could even find where the hunters were living. In town or some place outside of town?

Eventually, however, he decided to stay on the property and fortify the shed a bit more by using boards from the barn and loose bricks from the dilapidated house. He thought about switching from the shed to the barn and fortifying that too for a bit more room, but if people were searching for him, he would be easier to find in the barn than the shed. Of course, if people wanted him enough, they could simply burn everything down.

He ate lunch behind the shed, savoring the shade and a cool breeze kissing his sweaty face. He ate as much as he could, because it could very well be his last meal. In the trees, squirrels played and birds sang without a care in the world. A little jealous, Lon smiled. Ah, to be a carefree squirrel or bird. Just living your life. Living free.

A sigh fell out of him, and he finished his lunch, which was tuna from a can on white bread. No mayo or anything, which made the thing kind of bland. Still, it was his lunch. He made it himself. Like free people did. His thoughts drifted to the Old Man. Was he involved with the gameshow too? The more Lon thought about it the less likely it seemed. The Old Man was a bastard on so many levels, but he wasn't that much of a bastard.

He walked to the hydrant, drank deeply, and ventured into the house. Maybe there was a knife or something in there he could use for self-defense. The floor creaked and groaned under him as he moved deeper into the house. He avoided the side with the collapsed roof. There was a living room, furniture and all. There were rat and mouse infested recliner and couch. On the floor was a broken TV. A doll blanketed in black mold slumped near the broken TV.

The stench in the house was old, damp wood, mold, and something severely musty.

The kitchen was a biohazard of a mess. Shit and piss everywhere. Some of it was human. There were beer bottles, wine bottles and a few small plastic bottles of Fireball whiskey. Under the kitchen table, which was somehow still standing, there was a moldy and dusty sleeping bag and grungy old pillow. The stink of the room went deeper than the shit and piss. The reek of illness permeated the air from the walls and floor. From the very essence of the room.

Lon gagged and searched the drawers. Eventually, he found a rusty steak knife. Better than nothing. He hurried out of the house before he vomited. The place stank, but it was more than that. The very air, especially in the kitchen, was toxic. Something else lived there and it wasn't human. Something dark…

He took a few breaths of fresh air and spared a long look around. The sensation of something wrong still hadn't left him. Someone or something was watching him. Or it could be he was merely on edge and—

A tiny flash of light caught his peripheral. He spun and faced the thick forest where the flash came from. A frown crawled along his bearded face. His eyes shifted back and forth in their sockets, gaze trying to find the thing that didn't belong in the sea of green. But try as he might… all he saw was green leaves. Green weeds. Tall green grasses. A wall of fucking green.

Lon shook his head and glanced away. A dull ache spread from his temples and across his forehead. They were watching him. There was no doubt about it now. That was where the sense of wrongness stemmed from. They were watching.

They knew where he was staying. Likewise, they probably watched him fortify the shed. They, whoever they really were, knew everything.

"Fuck," he said, tone gruff. Tears welled in his eyes as the revelation dawned on him.

He glanced down, found a softball sized rock, pried it from the ground and chucked it in the direction of the flash.

"Leave me alone," he cried. His voice, which he rarely had to use over the years, squeaked at the end of alone.

Somewhere in the forest, a few birds chirped.

"I just want to be free!"

He staggered backward, breathing heavily, and wiped sweat from his forehead. Maybe he needed to find a different place to hide? No. They would follow him. He wasn't free. No matter how much he felt like he was earlier. He wasn't free and they wouldn't let him be free.

Both weariness and sorrow swallowed him. Lon shuffled toward the shed, head lowered, defeated. He would lie down in the shed, door wide open, and just let those hunters kill him. He had fought long enough. Maybe it was just his time now. Maybe best to just get it over with.

He stood inside the shed and stared at his little bed in the far corner, at the small stores of food in the other corner. He turned to the covered window and the fortified door. All useless efforts. All in vain.

A long, heavy sigh blew out of him.

Then a sudden realization surfaced in his mind through all the sorrow.

They wouldn't do anything while he was human.

That's not what they wanted.

They wanted a dog fight.

They wanted a monster to defeat.

Lon shook his head and stepped back outside. He gave the spot where the flash happened a glance and grunted.

They wanted a show, huh? Well, he would give them a show…

Lon turned toward town and began running.

CHAPTER 21

IF THOSE BASTARDS at the gameshow wanted to play him, he might as well fight back. And when the dog took over, he would stay awake and coach the creature.

He didn't have a plan, per se, but it was better than giving up. He had fought his entire life, and he wasn't about to lie down now. If he was going to die, he'd go down biting and clawing.

Lon slipped into town, bypassing a couple Sheriff vehicles and darting into a narrow alley between two brick buildings. He kicked a couple glass beer bottles out of the way and peeked around the corner. Downtown wasn't as bustling as he thought it would be. Instead, it was rather barren. A couple of people walked the sidewalks, but other than that...

The sun held fast at mid afternoon, and the day

was still sweltering. He wiped sweat from his face and glanced around. There were drones out and about. He had no doubt about it. But, as far as he could tell they weren't following him now. But just because he couldn't see them didn't mean they weren't buzzing around nearby waiting for him to step out into the open.

He drew in a breath, held it and hurried onto the sidewalk to the closest store. Which happened to be a shoe shop. He stumbled a bit and blinked at an older woman wearing large glasses behind a desk. Deeper into the shop was a man kneeling down in front of another man sitting in a chair holding a work boot. Everyone stared at him like he was some unnamable thing from the void.

Lon smiled. "Hi."

But nobody replied. The older woman frowned at him, as if searching for his soul or something.

Finally, she said, "Can I help you?"

Lon, trying to keep his smile, wiped his sweaty forehead and chuckled. "It's hot out there."

The woman's frown deepened. "Yeah."

He groped for more words to say, but it had been so long since he'd had real human contact and all he could do was shrug and turn to a wall of shoes. He stared at the shoes for a while. He nodded, as if he knew what he was looking for.

"Um," the lady behind the desk said. "Do you have a wife or daughter you're looking at shoes for?"

Lon frowned and snorted. He shook his head and looked at her. "No. I... I'm not married."

The lady took her glasses off. "Then why are you looking at the women's shoes?"

Lon opened his mouth and closed it. He glared at the shoes for a second or two and shot a smile at the lady.

"Sorry." He moved toward the door. "I'll just—"

"Our men's section is back here," the man fitting the other man with a work boot said. "You lookin' for work or pleasure?"

Lon, lost again for words, nodded.

The man chuckled. "We got a couple walls back here. Come take a gander while I'll help you after this idiot figures out covering his little tootsies in the lumberyard."

"Says the guy who pisses himself every time the leaves fall," the man in the chair said.

Both men chuckled as Lon gradually made his way to the men's shoe section.

"Wouldn't be gettin' new boots if someone didn't take mine," the man in the chair said and shook his head. "The world is goin' to shit when someone steals another man's boots."

Lon blinked and stopped walking. He glanced down at the boots he wore. His eyes widened.

The shoe salesman snorted. "Maybe you shouldn't leave your boots on the porch." He winked at Lon.

"Listen, dickhead," the man in the chair said. "They were in my fuckin' house."

The shoe salesman shrugged. "Maybe it was a hobo then. Better boots than valuables, right?"

"That's…" the man in the chair sighed. "That's not the damn point and you know it. I swear, if you weren't my brother, I'd stomp your face in."

The shoe salesman chuckled. "You've been

saying that for like thirty years, bro, and still haven't done it."

"You just wait, *bro*," the other man said and faked a kick at the salesman.

Both men laughed and Lon hurried toward the door. If the man in the chair recognized the boots—

"Sir," the salesman said. "Did you see anything ya liked?"

Lon shook his head and was just opening the door when the man in the chair said, "Hey! I think those are my boots."

"What?" The salesman voice was a pitch higher than before. "You can't be serious."

"No," the other man said. "Those are my fuckin' boots. See my initials in yellow on the heel?"

"Oh… oh shit. Hey, mister, can you come back here and—"

Lon shot out of the shoe store and sprinted across the street, narrowly avoiding a large red truck. It gave a long honk and screech away as Lon darted into an adjacent alley. One even narrower than the last. Behind him the man Lon stole the boots from shouted all kinds of obscenities.

Coming to town was a mistake. He should have known it would be a—

A tall man with long black hair and wearing a tattered gray shirt and holey jeans stepped around the counter just as Lon came to the end of the alley.

They literally almost ran into each other.

The taller man cocked his head to the side, a frown spread along his grimy face. His nostrils flared and he drew in a deep breath. No more than a couple of seconds, his eyes widened.

Lon backed away a few feet and smiled. "Sorry. I
—"

A low growl emanated from the large man. A
man at least eight inches taller than Lon and five
times bulkier. Pure muscle by the look.

It took Lon only another handful of seconds to
realize who the man was.

The feral dog…

Lon held up his hands. "Hey. I'm not here to
fight. If you want this territory, it's yours. I'll leave."

The man grunted. A slight grin touched his thin
lips. Regardless, he did not speak. He only stepped
closer and closer.

"Fuck," Lon said. "Listen, I am not here to fight.
I will leave right now."

The man's grin faded as he continued to move
closer.

Lon was about to reiterate that he wasn't here to
fight and meant no harm, when he stopped himself.
The large man didn't understand him anyway. All
the man knew was survival and eliminating threats.
He was just as much a dog as his dog part was.
There would be no negotiating with him. No
compromising.

The man might as well have been a machine.

Lon spun and sprinted back through the alley
and almost crashed into the man he stole the boots
from. The feral man made a wild grab for him, but
Lon dodged the effort. Lon continued to back away
from the man. It was clear the feral man didn't care.
All he wanted to do was kill. Nothing else mattered.

Form the other end of the alley, the man from
the shoe shop shouted, "There he is! Motherfucker!

Give me my boots back! Already called the Sheriff!"

Lon glanced over his shoulder at the man running toward him then returned his attention to…

The feral man was gone.

Lon sighed, spared another glance over his shoulder at the man running at him, turned and sprinted out of the alley.

CHAPTER 22

He EVENTUALLY LOST the man chasing him for the boots and hid in a small, abandoned warehouse all the way across town.

The warehouse hadn't been abandoned for long, however, because there were still items on the shelves. One of the pallets was packed with potato chips. He ripped through the plastic wrap, pulled out a bag and opened it. The aroma filled his mouth with saliva. He ate lunch so wasn't starving, but the day was leaning into dinner time, or close to it, so…

Lon munched on potato chips as he walked around the warehouse. Coming to town turned out to be a massive mistake. Now the Sheriff was looking for him too.

He found a partial pallet of bottled water and grabbed one of the bottles on his way. By the time he made his way to the far end of the warehouse, the last of the warm water trickling down his throat, he knew what he would do.

Run. Just leave the town and run as far as he could from it. He wouldn't be able to do it during daylight so would have to wait until the dog part woke up. The only problem was how hot the inside of the warehouse was. For walking around in the building for a short time, it was like being trapped in a massive oven. He didn't want to step outside just in case someone spotted him but staying inside the warehouse might cook him alive.

Okay, probably not, but it could make him sick. He had water, but it was warm water and wouldn't do much to cool him down.

He strolled to the rear of the building where the loading docks were. Next to the large doors of the docks was a walk-in door. Lon opened it and the hinges gave a shrill squeal. He winced as the noise echoed throughout the warehouse. A breeze swirled in through the open door. A warm breeze, but ten times cooler than inside of the warehouse. The back of the warehouse faced a gravel lot and beyond that a a bunch of trees that could be more forest. He stood in the doorway, savoring the breeze as it cooled his sweaty skin.

So far, he didn't see a drone or any weird flashes in the woods. The lot itself, with its scatterings of weeds sprouting up through the gravel, was a sad, barren thing. There were a few rusty dumpsters slumped like ancient beasts at the far-right corner of the lot. He propped the door open with a cinderblock and backed away a bit. The breeze just barely touched him and was hardly felt in the old brick and steel oven he stood in.

Lon wiped sweat away, grabbed a few warm bottles of water and returned to the door. He took a swig, grimaced and was about to have another drink, when a slight crackling sound drifted to his ears. He frowned and lowered the bottle from his mouth. The crackling continued for a couple of seconds, then stopped.

He backed away from the propped open door and glanced around for something he could use as a weapon. All he could find was a scoop shovel. Better than nothing. His hands gripped the handle. Sweat dripped off the tip of his nose and trickled down the small of his back. He waited.

Eventually the crackling sound of shoes on gravel started up again. Closer and closer.

A dull chuckle floated through the foot wide gap of the open door.

Lon's body trembled. Without even seeing the person, he knew it was the tall, feral man he nearly ran into in the alley. He broke out of his reverie and kicked the cinderblock out of the doorway. The door slammed shut with a loud clank. He turned the deadbolt and backed away from the door again.

Nothing happened for a long time. Long enough for the shadows to change in the warehouse as the sun moved into the setting position.

Then… three slow knocks came from the door.

Lon gripped the shovel, sweaty hands squeaking on the wooden handle. He waited a while, but no more knocks came.

He relaxed a bit. The feral man couldn't get in here. He…

Lon's eyes widened. Except for the lobby door he entered from.

"Shit," he said, turned and ran across the warehouse to the lobby, heart jackhammering.

The feral man wasn't in the lobby, not anywhere outside from what Lon could see. A shiver passed through him as he locked the lobby doors and backed away. There were probably other exits he should check, but now, he couldn't move. The man scared him more than the dog part. There was something so cruel and monstrous about the man part. Something... evil. The feral man enjoyed toying with his prey. And there was no doubt in Lon's mind that the feral man was toying with him.

He wiped sweat off his face and returned to the main part of the warehouse. He drank another bottle of warm water and stared longingly at the door. Every part of him wanted to unlock it and prop it open with the cinderblock again. Because, while it wasn't exactly air conditioning, like... at all, the touch of breeze, while warm, was still a few degrees cooler than the inside of the old building.

The only hope he had was nightfall. The dog would wake up and he would instruct him to run away from the town, the gameshow and the feral man. Away from it all as far as he could run all night. He would have to cover his scent to keep the feral dog from tracking him. Somehow. The main goal was to get as far away from the town as possible.

He found a filthy office with a small window. Much too small for the feral man to climb through. It was too damn hot to care anyway. He opened the window, and a strong breeze struck his dripping face. He shivered. Once again, the breeze wasn't exactly cool, but a hell of a lot cooler than inside the building. Lon sighed, letting the breeze sooth him for a while.

The feral man didn't try to get in through the small window, nor did Lon hear or see the man. Maybe he had better things to do. It was a nice thought, but Lon doubted it. The feral man would be back. He liked to toy with his prey, after all.

Lon sat in front of the small window, relishing the warm breeze, drinking his fourth bottle of tepid water, and watched the sun sink below the tree line. The air whispering through the window cooled a bit and he closed his eyes. The relief caressed his very being for that singular beautiful moment in time.

He drew in a breath and blew it out slowly as the dog part of him began to stir.

CHAPTER 23

THE HUMAN PART of Lon made sure he was outside before the change happened and when the dog woke up, the first thing he heard was the nightly orchestra of frogs and crickets.

Lon shuddered, stood on his hind legs, and stretched. His spine crackled and his lungs opened up. He sucked in a deep breath, filling those larger lungs, and blew it all out slowly. He glanced around, not sure where he was. The human part left the shed. So where…

Run, the human part shouted at him. *You need to run away from town! Now!*

Lon shook his vulpine head. His gaze drifted back and forth. His stomach groaned for food. His first impulse was to find something to eat, but the human part was so insistent.

You can eat on the way! You need to run away before—

"Here, doggie, doggie…" A giggle echoed through the trees on Lon's left.

He recognized the voice right away. The woman with the uzis. Em. So, the feral dog didn't kill them after all. But why?

A deep growl trembled the air to his left, and he caught the faintest of wild stenches. He also knew that stench. From out of a large bush, the feral dog approached him on all fours, head lowered.

They laid a trap for him.

His heart bashed against his ribs. He glanced from the dog to Em as she skipped out of the woods.

A gentle click directly behind him.

Lon turned to find the woman with the crossbow grinning at him. Kelly? Yeah, something like that. She aimed the crossbow at him.

"End of the line," Kelly said.

"Wait," Em said. "I don't see any drones." She looked around. "Didn't they know where we'd be?"

Kelly shrugged. "Fuck'em."

"But we're being paid to—"

"I told you before," Kelly said. "I don't care about that. I don't give a shit about the show or getting paid." She leveled the crossbow at Lon. "I'm gonna kill this dog and when I'm done, I'll put an arrow in that big bastard over there."

The feral dog's growl deepened. Yes, the beast understood everything. It wasn't as dumb as it seemed. Lon turned to the other dog and, for a couple seconds, their gaze locked. For those fleeting seconds, Lon felt a connection. An understanding. He didn't trust the feral dog… but…

"Oh," Em said and laughed. "There's a drone. They found us!"

Kelly sighed, though didn't say anything.

For a minute or two, no one moved.

"Well," Kelly said finally. "Let's put these dogs down, then."

Em snorted and pointed her uzis at Lon. "One hundred percent."

Lon glowered at the woman. His muzzle curled into a snarl. He caught the feral dog stop in his peripheral.

"Do like we planned," Kelly said.

"Gotcha," Em said. Her grin glimmered under the pale glow of a pregnant moon.

Overhead, several drones buzzed back and forth. A few circled slowly.

Lon tried to ignore the damn things and focus on Em. But it was more than just her. Kelly was behind him and the feral dog glared at him from the right. He was trapped. The other problem was how the hunger gnawed at his guts. He needed food and he needed it now.

He ducked, though not fast enough to avoid the first spray of bullets from Em. Bullets struck his chest and shoulders, and he roared as he plowed into her. He slammed her to the ground, swept a claw at her face, and cleaved most of her lower jaw off. She wailed, tongue flailing in the gory hole that used to be the front of her face. She fired the uzis wildly while her body thrashed under him.

Several stabs of pain riddled his back. Lon yelped, stuffed some of Em's face into his maw and ate it. Just as he swallowed, the feral dog pounced.

The dog crashed into Lon and knocked him off Em but didn't tear into him. Instead, the feral dog kicked Em's thrashing body at Lon and darted away. The feral dog disappeared into the night before Kelly could take a shot. Lon tore off Em's right arm and ate as much as he could before Kelly shot him again. He yanked the arrow out of his forearm and growled at Kelly.

She glared at him and loaded another arrow. "This arrow is special." She pulled the string back. "Too heavy to load into my auto cylinders, though."

Em, still alive, shrieked as Lon tore a large chunk out of her lower torso with his claw and slurped it down. He needed it. He needed energy and healing. Blood drizzled down his furry chin as he watched Kelly move to the right. He bared his teeth at her.

"You can growl at me all you want, motherfucker," she said. "But you die tonight."

He tore more out of Em's torso, clawing out organs and stuffing them into his mouth. He chewed and swallowed... chewed and swallowed.

She aimed the crossbow at him.

Lon slid to the left and tackled Kelly. She didn't scream and immediately began stabbing him in the side with a knife. It was painful, but not enough to stop him. He smacked the crossbow out her hand and stood. She roared and stabbed wildly at his legs.

Without hesitation, he reached down, grabbed her head like a professional basketball player would a ball, and lifted her to her feet. She grunted, grasping his forearms and trying to get free of his grip. She stabbed his arms with the knife, eventually severing a tendon that made his hand loosen on her head.

Kelly dropped to the ground and rolled away before he could kill her.

Behind him, Em, still alive, began to sob.

Kelly swept her crossbow off the ground, rolled to the side and pointed it at Lon.

"Nice try, dog," she said. "Now eat shit."

He lunged before she could pull the crossbow's trigger, flaying her face. She yowled, staggered backward and fired. The arrow missed and tore off the arm holding the crossbow. And, finally, Kelly screamed.

Lon tossed the severed arm aside, though not before taking a bite. Kelly, still screaming, drew a pistol and fired two rounds point blank into his chest. He yelped and leaped backward. Those hurt. Really hurt. They were still hurting.

A craggy chuckle drew Lon's attention back to Kelly. She grinned as blood dribbled down her chin. "Gotcha, motherfucker." She swayed and glanced at the ragged remains of the arm he tore off then she glared at one of the drones. "Get medical in here and take care of my arm. I won."

The drone buzzed a few feet from her head.

"You hear me? I wo—"

A hole about the size of a quarter appeared directly between her wide eyes. Her mouth opened wide. Her lower jaw jittered. The drone near her head slowly backed away while her knees buckled, and she dropped to the ground. Steam slithered out of the hole in her forehead.

Lon glanced behind him in the direction of the bullet that killed Kelly.

I think they have a sniper, the human part of Lon said. *Get inside!*

But Lon's movements were slow and disjointed. His vision blurred and he shook his head. Everything around him appeared to be floating in water. He shook his head again, but the floating didn't stop. His stomach lurched and he shuffled toward the warehouse lobby doors. Whatever Kelly shot him with… they weren't normal bullets.

He caught a slight flash from the woods. Much like the one the human part saw earlier near the shed.

He stumbled into the lobby doors, yanked one open and collapsed half in and half out of the lobby. His arms and legs wouldn't work right, but he managed to drag himself all the way into the lobby. A low whine wheezed out of Lon's mouth. It was like all the energy was leeching out of him and his body set on fire. He struggled to claw his way toward the door to the warehouse when all his strength evaporated, and he fell still on the floor. His vision darkened then went black and he knew now more.

THE DOG FOUNDATION

"HEY," DOUG SAID, shaking Randy awake. "Something is wrong."

Randy groaned, head throbbing, vision blurry. His mouth and throat were too dry and all he managed was a thin squeak.

Doug rolled his eyes and said, "Mike? Mike, he's drunk as hell over here."

"Goddamn it," Mike said and shook Randy hard enough to snap some of the boozy haze out of him long enough for Randy to wave Micheal away.

"We have a problem, asshole," Jeff said from somewhere nearby. "It's the fuckin' pilot and you're drunk off your ass right now?"

Randy tried, he really did, to sit up and acknowledge what was going on, but in the end only slumped in his chair and mumbled something even he didn't understand. Except for the throbbing pain in his head, his body was numb.

"Oh, for fuck sake," Jeff said. "This isn't good."

"What do we do?" Doug said. "If this bombs…"

"Everyone out," Micheal said. "I'm gonna have a chat with Randy here."

"Why do we have to leave?" Jeff said. "I think —"

"Fine," Micheal said in a calm tone. "Stay. Doesn't matter."

Randy drifted in and out of consciousness. Micheal stood nearby, but the man was so blurry Randy had to close his eyes or he would puke all over.

"Hey, Randy," Micheal said. "Are our names attributed to the pilot in any way?"

Randy snorted, turned onto his side in the chair.

"He's too fucked up," Doug said.

Micheal gave Randy a rough shake. "Are our names on any documentation involving the pilot?"

Randy waved a hand at the man. Everything began to spin. "Jus'on… on 'proval."

"Just on the initial approval?"

Randy nodded. Well, at least he thought he nodded. His stomach churned and vomited.

"Goddamn it," Jeff said. "Got it on my shoes."

Randy chuckled and rolled onto his other side.

"So," Doug said. "We're not linked financially to this… thing?"

"No," Micheal said. "Initial approval is just that. We approved but hold no stake in the show."

"The motherfucker was going to stiff us," Jeff said. "He'd get paid big if the show's a hit but we'd lose out."

Randy glutted vomit onto the floor and began fading out again. They were in for a surprise if the show went to hell.

"Get Don and the guys to take Randy for a walk," Micheal said after a long pause.

No one said anything and Randy couldn't hold onto consciousness any longer and fell into the dark void of drunkenness.

He woke up a bit a little later. Cool air touched his cheeks, waking him up a little more. He glanced around through his boozy daze. He focused on the weathered boards under his...

"What..." Randy said through the daze. "W'goin' on?"

"Oh, Mr. Wellman," a gentle voice said. "Nothing to worry about."

Randy smiled and blacked out again.

When he woke again, his hands were handcuffed behind his back and his legs wrapped together with heavy chains.

He blinked and squinted at his surroundings. His vision was still too blurry to really see anything. Too swimmy with booze.

"Wh... what's this?"

No one answered.

Gradually, his vision cleared enough to for his brain to at least recognize he was in the back seat of a car.

Randy shook his head. "What... what the fuck?"

Then he finally noticed the smell. A very familiar odor. One that reminded him of his grandpa at the gas station filling gas cans for the mower or boat, or just topping off his truck's tank. A smell he liked when he was a kid and brought back good memories with his grandpa. That smell didn't do any of that right now, though. Because the more he moved around, the more he realized his clothes were soaked.

Drenched in gasoline.

Even in his drunken stupor, he understood what was happening. His heart hammered and he scooted to the closest back door. He turned and pulled the handle, but the door wouldn't open.

"No," he managed and scooted to the other door. But just like the other one, it refused to open.

His breath grew heavier, and he moved toward the front seats. If he could just…

Two pistols pressed against either temple.

"Settle down, Mr. Wellman," an icy voice said. "I just need a signature."

Randy frowned. His head was still swimmy and beginning to hurt.

One of the pistols lifted away from his temple and a tablet with a signature space was placed between the seats.

"I'm going to take the handcuffs off, Mr. Wellman." A different voice from the last. This one sounded more cordial. Gentler. "And I want you to sign the document."

Randy, still frowning, shook his head. "What is it?"

"No questions," the colder man said. "Just sign it."

Randy opened his mouth to protest, but the cordial man stopped him.

"All you have to do is sign it, Mr. Wellman. No

questions. Then we'll let you go."

Randy, still drunk and his brain not firing on all cylinders, snorted. "I'm not gonna sign shom'thin I don't know 'bout."

"I'll say this only once," the cordial man said. "Sign the document without question and we will let you go. If you do not… well… I'm sure you smell the gasoline…"

It took Randy almost a minute for all that to sink in. He blinked.

"Y-You're gonna kill me?"

Without hesitation, the colder man said, "Yep."

"Mr. Wellman," the cordial man said. "I am going to take the handcuffs off now. Either you sign the document after I do, or yes… you will die."

A shiver shook Randy. His booze addled mind finally connected all the dots. He opened his mouth, about to ask again what the document was, and closed it before any words were uttered.

The passenger back door opened and large man wearing a white dress shirt with rolled up sleeves and a buzz cut reached in and took the handcuffs off.

"Okay," the man said, backed out of the car and shut the door. He returned to the passenger seat, turned and tapped the tablet. "Now go ahead and sign, Mr. Wellman. Let's put this behind us. Sound good?"

Randy sighed, picked up the stylus, and signed in the digital box.

The man in the passenger seat grunted and took the tablet away. "Good. Thank you, Mr. Wellman."

Both men got out of the car and shut their doors

in tandem.

Randy waited for one of the back doors to open, but they didn't.

"Um," Randy said and wiped sweat from his face with trembling hands. "Hello?"

Neither man responded.

He tried either door but as before, they wouldn't open. His heart quickened and he squeezed through the gap between the front seats and crawled into the driver's seat. Randy reached for the door handle.

"Oh, Mr. Wellman," the cordial man said from the partially opened passenger window.

Randy blinked at the man and the man smiled.

"Have a nice night."

The man flicked a Zippo alight and tossed it onto Randy's lap. The gasoline fumes caught nearly at once.

"No," Randy cried. He began taking off his shirt and the Zippo slipped off his lap and plopped onto the floor, which caught fire with a low *floof* sound.

Blue flames sprawled along the car floor, crawled up the seats and Randy's legs. He screamed as the fire seared his skin. Using his shirt, he tried to put out the flames burning through his pants and the shirt caught fire in a wild blaze. He flung the burning shirt, and it landed on the passenger seat, which soon exploded into flames.

Randy screamed and tried ramming the driver's door with his shoulder. It didn't budge. Still screaming, he crawled into the backseat to escape the fire, but the fire followed him. He kicked at the windows as the fire engulfed him. Shrieking, he kicked and kicked and…

The window finally shattered, and he managed to wriggle partially through before he got stuck at his shoulders and chest.

He wailed and struggled but to no avail.

The inside of the car soon became an inferno.

Randy screamed until his body fell into shock and he fell limp, arms dangling, burnt and bleeding fingers dancing at the night air.

Eventually he stopped moving and the fire consumed him.

CHAPTER 24

LON WOKE, FINDING himself still in the lobby. Only a foot or so from the door to the warehouse.

He groaned and scrambled to his feet. A growl trembled in his throat that soon turned into a jet of vomit. Lon's legs quivered and he dropped to all fours. Whatever Kelly shot him with was—

"She poisoned you," a gruff, very familiar voice said from the far shadows.

Lon backed away, eyes widening as Master stepped into the moonlight. Not a tall man, but beefy and imposing, nonetheless. His frown deeply lined his pale, sweaty face.

The man chuckled. "You're probably wonderin' why I'm here." He shrugged and glanced toward the glass doors of the lobby. "You're still m'dog." He grinned at Lon. "Still my property."

Lon growled and paced back and forth.

Master waved a dismissive hand. "Oh, stop that. They don't know I'm here."

Lon glared at the man. Every ounce of him wanted to rip Master apart and eat as much as he could. But whatever Kelly poisoned him with was still affecting his thoughts. Even the human part wasn't making any sense.

"That bitch laced those bullets with chocolate," Master said. "Her other arrows were laced with it too." He stepped closer to Lon, though not too close, and shook his head. "Makes ya sick but won't kill ya."

Master grunted, brought out a chair from behind the desk, and sat down in front of Lon. He sighed and the man's angry demeanor melted some. "Son… I'm sorry. I don't say that much, but I am. I'm sorry."

The hunger clouded Lon's thoughts off and on.

"I know the human part of you in there can understand." Master snorted and shook his head. "Been fightin' dogs since I was in m'twenties. Turned seventy y'sterday." He looked directly at Lon. "Long time. A long time and a lot of money." Sat forward a bit. "And too many good dogs like you killed for entertainment's sake." He leaned back and the chair creaked. "I'm done with it all, kid, and I put in place things that'll end the fights."

Lon growled, trying to fight the hunger.

"I'm sorry, Lon," Master said. He smiled. It was the first time Lon saw the man smile and it took him aback a bit. "I know it's not gonna make up for the years of hell I put ya through, but I am sincerely sorry."

Lon staggered.

"You're hungry," Master said. The man nodded. "I figured you'd be. That's why I want you to eat me."

Lon blinked.

"They got them drones everywhere," Master said. "They're waitin' for ya. Probably on a commercial break. Ya also got a sniper out there. Smart, but one cold hearted bastard if I ever saw one. Met'im the other day before he went off into the woods. Lon, he will torture you before killing you. The other dog out there…" Master waved a hand. "Y'all might be able to join up to kill that bastard. It's feral so I dunno." Master smiled again. "I see ya swayin', son."

Master brought out a pocketknife, thumbed the blade out, and slashed his left wrist. Blood streamed onto the dusty floor.

The sweet scent struck Lon like an anvil. His nostrils flared, drawing it in. Savoring it.

"I know it never felt like it," Master said. "But I considered you my son. I loved you like my son."

Lon pounced, the hunger taking full control, and buried his teeth into Master's sweaty throat. Blood sprayed into his mouth and down his throat. He nearly gagged then swallowed quickly. Master made a thick gurgling sound but didn't fight. Instead, the man wrapped his arms around Lon in a firm embrace.

By the time the hunger was sated, most of Master was eaten.

Lon roared, anger overtaking everything else, and burst through one of the lobby windows and into the night.

CHAPTER 25

DRONES SCATTERED LIKE FLIES.

Lon sniffed the air, searching for the sniper. But all he caught were the scents of deer and Master.

He wanted to sprint back to town, but the sniper was his main target, and the human part told him the sniper wouldn't have moved away yet.

Lon moved into the woods, nostrils drawing in all the scents. From the mushrooms growing on the fallen tree to the bear lumbering a few hundred feet away. He moved in a slow zigzag, changing directions in the hope of catching the sniper's scent.

No such luck, though.

With the taste of Master's blood still on his tongue, Lon turned toward the town.

No, the human part shouted. *We need to run away!*

Lon growled. There would be no more running.

It ended tonight.

One way… or another.

CHAPTER 26

THE TOWN WAS bustling, considering it was nighttime. People walked the streets of downtown and if not for the guns in their hands, Lon would have thought there was a festival or something going on.

Almost every man and woman carried a gun. There were no kids out and about tonight. Which was a good and bad thing. Good that they weren't walking around town at the sides of their armed parents… bad, because they might be home alone, and anything could happen…

The town's people were taking justice into their own hands.

Every now and then, he caught a drone zip around before disappearing.

They knew where he was.

The show people knew, but not the townspeople.

Maybe he could—

"Residents of Dyer," a loud voice boomed throughout the town.

The people with guns stopped walking and looked around.

Run, the human part of Lon said. *Run before…*

"There is a werewolf stalking your town," the booming voice said. "Yes. It's true. A werewolf is hunting your children! Right now!" The voice roared, hurting Lon's ears. "It's peeking through your windows. It's going to sneak inside your homes and eat your babies!"

More than a few people gasped.

A couple across the street from Lon glanced at each other and hurried out of sight to the left.

Lon slipped back into the deeper shadows of the alley. More people began to scatter. Most probably running to their children.

For a second or two, Lon relaxed a bit. With all of them returning to their homes it would make it easier to find the sniper or even the feral dog.

The feral dog…

Why did he leave Lon that woman Em when he could have eaten her himself? Was there a form of respect there? Maybe he—

"The dog, the werewolf," the booming voice said. "Is hiding in the alley near the US Bank."

Lon's body stiffened. His eyes widened in their sockets.

I told you to run, the human part spat at him.

"I see it," a woman shouted from the sidewalk in front of the alley. She pointed directly at Lon. "By the dumpster!"

Lon's ears laid back a bit. His tail curled up. A low whine filled his throat. He rarely every got scared, but he was now. There were so many angry people. So many of them with guns.

A few men with what appeared to be AR-15s crowded around the woman and followed her gaze until they saw Lon crouched in the alley.

"Holy shit," one of the men shouted. "It's huge!"

"I got'im," another of the men said aiming his rifle at Lon. "Get the trophy ready boys!"

Lon's paralysis broke and he darted behind the dumpster a millisecond before the man fired is gun. The bullet ricochets off the brick wall, spraying red dust, and struck the wall next to Lon and the dumpster. Only about a foot away.

"It's a quick bastard," the man yelled. "Move in! Shoot t'kill!"

Lon spun and, keeping the dumpster between him and the mob, sprinted down the alley. A few gunshots rang out but missed him. He sprang out of the alley, cut left, crossed the street and leaped into someone's back yard. He scaled the house to the roof and rested while the mob, which was more than the few men now, scattered out of the alley.

He pressed himself against the shingles while the mob searched for him.

"Where'd it go?" Someone shouted.

"Might be 'round Mills by now," another shouted back.

"Mills is a mile away, idiot," another said.

"Check all the yards," someone else said. This guy sounded like he was more of a leader. Firm, assertive, strong voice. "Y'all got the description of the beast. Shoot to kill. This fucker is fast so if you get a shot, take it."

Lon watched the men search the front and back yard of the house he hid on and the yards surrounding the house. Eventually, they moved away from the area.

Lon climbed back down and slipped through the shadows toward the shed while keeping all of his senses in tune for the sniper. A scent that differed from everything else and the people of the town. The small flash in the darkness like he saw in the woods near the shed and again near the old warehouse.

His human part screamed at him to run as fast and as far as he could before morning.

But, even with the town fully aware of him now, the feral dog and sniper, Lon wouldn't run. One way or another, it ended tonight.

He made it out of town without being noticed and approached his shed.

He caught movement on his right, but too late to stop the attack.

The feral dog crashed into Lon, knocking him off his feet, and slammed him to the ground. The dog roared into Lon's face. The breath was hot and vile and angry. Lon roared back and shoved the feral dog off him.

The other dog shook his head and snorted as Lon stood. He growled and glanced at something over Lon's shoulder. Lon, not fully trusting the feral dog, risked a quick glance behind him and instantly caught a drone hovering above the barn.

Lon looked at the feral dog and grunted.

The feral dog circled Lon, a deep growl gurgling in his throat. Lon growled in return, though confused. Did the feral dog want to kill or help him? A couple more drones zipped around like hummingbirds.

Before Lon could react, the feral dog pounced, driving him back to the ground. Lon shoved him off again and… again, the feral dog circled.

He's on our side, the human part of Lon said. *He's just putting on a show for the cameras.*

Lon a growled and the feral dog growled back.

The feral dog winked and launched himself at Lon, but instead of striking Lon, he snatched a drone out of the air with his jaws. He bashed it against the shed until it was nothing but plastic splinters and looked at something above Lon's head.

Lon glanced up, saw the drone, and plucked it out of the air. He slammed it to the ground and stomped on it.

The feral dog nod and Lon nodded in return.

Oh, the human part said. *Yes, destroy the drones and the gameshow people won't be able to see what's happening.*

The feral dog sprinted across the yard, scrambled up the house and plucked another drone out of the air. He landed and clawed the drone apart.

Movement in front of Lon, near the woods. He rushed forward, leaped and clamped down onto the drone with his teeth. He tore it apart and tossed it into the weeds still sparking.

The other two drones still hovering about zipped away into the darkness.

The feral dog glanced at Lon. They shared a nod, and the feral dog ran into the woods where he disappeared. It was like a good-bye. Maybe it was.

Lon turned toward the shed.

Heat sliced through the top of his shoulder. Lon grunted and dropped to all fours. He sniffed the air and of course didn't catch a scent that differed from everything else. The sniper was out there and even better than Kelly at masking their scent and hiding. Lon moved toward the shed and a smoking hole appeared in the ground an inch in front of his claw. He didn't even hear the shot. The sniper also knew how to mask the sound of gunshots too.

Lon turned toward the house and another smoking hole appeared in the ground an inch in front of him.

It was clear. The sniper had him and let him know it.

Lon's gaze scanned the yard, the house, the…

A tiny flash winked at him from the top of the barn. Lon's eyes narrowed. The human part told him the sniper knew he knew where the sniper was now.

A white light snapped into existence on top of the barn, illuminating the sniper. A man with long hair tied into a ponytail, straddling the gable of the barn with the rusty rooster weathervane. He grinned and aimed his rifle at Lon.

Lon started forward, the man slowly shook his head, and Lon stopped.

He's got us, the human part said. *It's over.*

Lon sighed and stood upright. He glared directly at the sniper.

Yes… it would end tonight.

One way or another.

He did not close his eyes and bared his teeth in a snarl.

So be it…

The sniper peered into his scope.

Lon's heart thudded heavily. Louder and louder until it was the only sound in the world. A slow, deep thud-thud-thud. A soothing sound that would lull him to sleep before the sniper put a bullet in it and ended the sound indefinitely. Before…

The feral dog rose up behind the sniper. A hulking dark figure, claws splayed. His eyes gleamed in the sniper's light.

It took a second, at least, before the sniper's head lifted away from the scope and a frown creased his face. A low growl rose in the cool night air. A sound that would be barely audible to human ears, but extremely clear to Lon.

The sniper's face slackened, and his eyes widened as realization kicked in.

He was just beginning to turn around when the feral dog reached down and tore his throat out. He fired a shot from his rifle and grabbed at the gushing wound in his throat.

The feral dog twisted the sniper's head and ripped it from the man's convulsing body. Blood spouted and the sniper's body fell off the roof of the barn. It hit the ground with a dull thud. Lon grunted and looked at the roof.

The feral dog lifted the sniper's head in the air and howled. Long and loud.

Heart thundering, Lon reared back and howled too.

In town, all the dogs not like them whined. A few

even pissed on their owner's carpets.

Then they began to bark.

The barking wouldn't stop until dawn and by then it didn't matter anyway.

CHAPTER 27

LON LISTENED TO the dogs not like him bark from town.

Not far away, a coyote yowled.

It was sick, by the sound. Coyotes roamed in packs but this one was solitary. Which meant it was either sick or elderly and on the verge of death.

The feral dog cracked the sniper's head open, pried off the top of the skull and handed Lon the severed head.

Lon huffed and looked at the feral dog.

The other dog nodded and turned away. Was he surveilling the area or giving him privacy? Maybe it didn't even matter.

Lon scooped the sniper's brain out and ate it. The gray matter wasn't exactly tasty, but it was about respecting the feral dog. Besides, food was food and—

The feral dog spun around, lightning quick, and backhanded the Lon across the muzzle so hard Lon stumbled away and fell. His head was like a nest of angry wasps for a few seconds as the other dog loomed over him, teeth bared. A deep growl vibrated through the feral dog's broad chest. So, it was all a ploy. A game. The dog wanted to gain Lon's trust and helped eliminate the competition so he could have Lon all to himself. He fed Lon because he wanted Lon to be at peak strength.

So, there could be a real dog fight.

Lon stood, and even though the feral dog was taller and broader, the other dog moved backwards a few steps. Lon growled, revealing his teeth. His heart bashed against his ribs and his ears laid back. He had fought big dogs like the feral one, but they also trained and could be predictable.

The feral dog was unpredictable and appeared to be smarter than the other dogs.

Lon shifted to the right and the feral dog mimicked him. He moved to the left, and again, the other dog followed. Lon snorted. So, the feral dog didn't know how to fight. He was avoiding confrontation. So, then why did he start a fight with Lon? Didn't make any sense.

The feral dog lunged, slashing Lon across the face with his long claws. Lon yelped, spun away and swung back around. He dug deep grooves into the feral dog's stomach. The dog whined and stumbled away from Lon. He gaped at the gouges in his furry belly. Each one pursed like bloody lips.

The dogs in town barked. An owl hooted. The feral dog whined, and his gaze lifted from his stomach to Lon. Genuine hurt in those yellow tinged eyes. He staggered away a few more feet. Lon glanced at the wound and huffed. A gray loop of intestine peeked through one of the gouges.

The scratches on Lon's face itched as they began to heal, but the feral dog's wounds... weren't healing. At all.

Lon blinked and looked at the feral dog.

The dog grunted and dropped to his knees. He lowered his head, broad shoulders heaving. The feral dog couldn't heal himself. Or, if he could, it was much slower than Lon.

Lon relaxed a bit and straightened. He cocked his head to the side a bit. The other dog's entire body shook, and he lifted his head to look at Lon. Tears trembled in his eyes. He reached out. Lon sighed and shook his head, and the other dog lowered his arm. He whined at Lon and Lon nodded. The dog feral dog was dying.

Lon grunted, splayed his right claw and moved toward the feral dog. He would end the dog's misery. A mercy killing. He had to do a few of those during his years of fighting. Even if Master screamed at him not to and let the other dog suffer longer. But Master was dead, and the fights were bullshit and nothing, dog or otherwise, he should be made to suffer for entertainment. His gaze shifted to a stray drone hovering above his shed.

The feral dog launched himself into Lon and tackled him to the ground. The dog buried his teeth into the space between Lon's neck and shoulder. Lon yelped and knocked the feral dog off him. The dog ate the chunk of flesh it tore from Lon and leered at him on all fours. Blood drooled from between his teeth and down his furry chin. A couple more loops of intestines poked out of the slashes in his abdomen. But it was his eyes that unnerved Lon the most. The hate. The rage. The hunger. Those fiery, yellow eyes...

Then everything clicked into place. Lon backed away, claws splayed and ready, but his heart slammed in his throat. Fear clutched his bowels in its greasy grip. Fear, he hoped, the feral dog didn't sense.

It all fell back on territory. The feral dog had marked the town as his and Lon didn't run away. Didn't run, just like the human part told him to do. Maybe he should have ran, but...

Lon never ran from a fight.

He faced every fight headstrong. Even when he felt like he might be losing. He stood... and fought.

This fight was no different.

The feral dog circled Lon on all fours. A deep growl rumbled out of him. A single drone buzzed, moving in a little closer. Neither Lon nor the feral dog looked at it, though both knew it was there.

The show must go on...

Lon kept his attention on the other dog. Every now and then, the feral dog winced from the wound in his abdomen. Lon frowned. Why would the dog continue fighting with such a painful wound? What was there to prove, other than claiming a territory? Even then, the effort seemed fruitless.

The feral dog lunged, slashing a claw. Lon dodged the attack, swept to the right, dipped and tugged one of the loops of intestines, pulling a large section out. The feral dog yelped, scrambled away and frantically tried tucking his intestines back in.

The spot between Lon's shoulder and neck itched as the missing chunk healed back in.

The human part told Lon to stop. Told him to run away. Let the creature be. But the human part didn't fully understand the dog part, just as the dog part didn't fully understand the human part.

Lon ignored the yapping in his head and pounced on the feral dog. The other dog flung him away with a roar and lashed out with frantic sweeps of his long claws. Lon dodged every sweep and caught one of the claws between his teeth. Growling, he tore three fingers off and spat them onto the ground. The feral dog gasped and staggered backwards gaping at the three stumps. He glanced from the stumps to Lon and back again.

Gradually, the feral dog's muzzle wrinkled in a snarl. Those furious eyes settled on Lon once more. The dog sprang forward and slashed Lon across the chest. Lon leaped away, merely avoiding another attack, slipped to the side and rammed his right claw into the feral dog's abdominal wound.

The feral dog yowled. He reared back, body quaking. His gaze fell on Lon and Lon met it.

Lon straightened, claw still inside the dog, gaze still locked on the feral dog. The dog whined. Blood spewed from his yawning maw. Growled and ripped the feral dog's intestines out. The dog gagged, blinked and shoved Lon away. Intestines still in his claw, Lon grunted and yanked. Most of them plopped like dead gray snakes onto the dirt.

The feral dog yelped, body shuddering. He

dropped to his knees. A low whine filtered out of his mouth while he tried to stuff his intestines back in. Dirt and all.

Lon moved forward, both claws splayed. Time to end it. Then maybe he would run away from town. Maybe he—

He felt the searing pain spread along his back before he heard the gunshot.

Lon turned and a kid, a boy, holding a shotgun gasped.

"I-I'm sorry," the boy said, eyes wide. "I... I..." He shuffled backwards. "P-please don't hurt me."

A deep growl resonated through Lon's chest as the buckshot in his back healed.

The boy dropped the shotgun, still backing away. He held his arms up in surrender.

Lon surged forward and loomed over the boy. No older than sixteen.

The boy screamed, tripped over his own feet and fell to the ground. He scrambled and crawled away. Lon growled louder and the boy gained his feet and ran.

The feral dog rushed by Lon before he could stop him.

Lon's eyes widened. He sprinted behind the other dog, already knowing he was too late.

The feral dog ripped the boy's throat out just as Lon plowed into him. They tumbled into the road, claws slashing and gouging. Lon chomped down on the feral dog's forearm, catching it before the claw filleted his face open. He tore out a large chunk, ate it and shoved the other dog away from him.

Holding his intestines in one claw, the feral dog

snorted.

Lon's eyes widened as the intestines began slipping back inside.

The child, the human part said. *He needs to eat children to heal. That's why all the children went missing. He ate them…*

The wound slurped the intestines in like spaghetti noodles. And that was just from a bit of flesh from the boy.

Lon charged, severing the intestines from returning to the dog's body, and slammed the other dog to the ground. He clawed out the feral dog's throat and gripped the spinal cord. The dog gurgled and struggled to free himself from Lon's fatal grip. His claws slapped at Lon, but without conviction. Eventually, the feral dog's gaze shifted to the dead child. He reached for the corpse and Lon dragged him away. Not like the other dog could eat anything at the moment. Not with Lon's claw inside his throat and clutching his spine…

Lon leaned in close. He might be a monster in every other sense, but no matter how hungry he was, he'd never eat a child. He *couldn't* eat a child. How or why the feral dog could only eat kids to heal and for strength was beyond Lon. Even the human part didn't know.

The feral dog gurgled, eyes bulging from his sockets.

Lon growled, furious gaze meeting the feral dog's terrified gape, then he yanked the feral dog's head off… spine and all.

The body twitched for a for a few seconds and fell still. The head, on the other hand, nipped at

Lon's arm. With a roar, claw still gripping the spine, Lon swung turned and swung the feral dog's head into the stone foundation of the old house like a Medieval flail. The dog's skull cracked open. A second swing and the creature's brains splattered all over the stone foundation. Bits of skull struck Lon's legs.

Lon reared and released a long, wild howl at the night.

He tossed the spine and demolished head aside and glanced around.

The human part told him to run now. He was free. He…

No, he wasn't free. Not yet. Not as some gameshow freak.

Lon ran back toward town.

CHAPTER 28

HE SPOTTED THE drone hovering above the house where Lon first saw the aftermath of the feral dog. The mutilated bodies of the kids and all the blood flashed before his mind's eyes. He shook his head to clear it and focused on the drone. It was looking elsewhere, unaware of Lon's presence.

Lon slinked to the house, meaning to climb up the side when he was suddenly doused in bright light. He gasped, spun around and squinted. Try as he might, though, he couldn't see past the glare.

"There he is, folks," a man with a boisterous voice boomed. "The dog that killed your children!"

Lon's eyes widened.

A stream of silence followed. Then...

"You killed my Millie, you motherfucker," a woman cried from somewhere beyond the bright lights.

"Ladies and gentlemen," the boisterous voice was now crooning. "This is your chance for true justice. *Your* justice. We supplied you with the weapons you need." The voice paused for a couple heart beats. "Standing before you is the monster that stole your babies from you. Look, their blood still stains his fur! He's been a busy boy." Another pause. "Now, justice is served…"

White hot heat struck his right bicep. The gunshot shot followed a millisecond later. Lon blinked and glanced at his arm. He stared at the trickle of blood dripping from his bicep and returned his attention the bright lights.

The show must go on…

Lon shivered. How many were out there? How many guns were fixed on him? His heart lurched and knew there would be no way out of the situation. They would shoot him enough to where he'd be unable to heal. And unless he someone was close enough to take a bite out of…

He sighed. So, this was the end.

No, the human part said. *We fight. We fight to the death.*

Lon remembered when the human part wanted to run earlier. Which, thinking about it now, he was probably right. Maybe Lon should have ran and fought another day. Still, that's not how it worked out and Lon never felt so much pride for the human part than he did now. Not that they were ever at serious odds anyway. Disagreements, sure but—

Hot pain slammed into his chest. Another bullet. He yelped and dropped to a knee as the bullet was pushed out of his chest and the wound healed.

"Think I got'im," a man shouted. "Where's my money?"

There's only one way out of this, the human part said. *And I think you know what it is…*

Lon did.

A deep growl spread through his chest and filled his throat. His glare fixed on the bright lights.

"Uh, Carl?" A man said. "I don't think it's dead."

"Son of a bitch," another man said. "Well, let's put this dog down!"

A bunch of hoots and hollers followed.

Lon seized the moment and sprang forward.

"Oh, shit," someone cried.

Lon, on all fours, zipped back and forth as the gunfire began. A couple bullets caught him, but nothing serious. The closer he got to the large wall of bright lights, the more he was able to see slim dark spaces between them. He sprinted at one of those slim dark spaces and was about to jump when a buckshot sheared the right side of his face off.

Lon's head exploded in agony. He stumbled and fell, hitting the ground hard. His momentum carried him forward and he slid a few feet on the grass.

"Woo," someone shouted. "Ya see that? Took its damn face clean off!"

Lon grunted and struggled to lift himself off the ground. Just as he was getting to all fours, bright white pain slammed into his side, followed by a deep report. Lon flew through the air, rolled a bit, and laid still gaping at the night sky.

"Holy shit, Ed," a man said. "Ya brought your

goddamn elephant gun?"

"Didn't know what we were up against," Ed said.

"Aren't we supposed to use silver bullets?" A woman asked. "That's in all the stories, right?"

"Well, we weren't given silver bullets, *Ann*," a man said in a condescending tone. "Let the men handle this."

Meanwhile, Lon's face was mostly healed and the giant hole in his side had closed a bit. The bleeding stopped, though not fast enough. He lost too much blood and needed to feed again to regain his strength.

Play dead, the human part whispered.

Lon closed his eyes and didn't move as the mob inched closer and closer.

"Think that damn elephant gun did it, Ed," a man said. "It's not movin'."

"I'll be collecting the check then," Ed said and chuckled. "Them people watching?"

"Supposed t'be."

"Better share the wealth, Eddie," another man spouted.

"I don't have to share shit," Ed said. "And don't call me Eddie."

They were close now. Very close. Just a little more...

"How much ya think those guys will be payin'?"

"Thought they said five million," a woman said.

"Nah," a man said. "Probably a million."

"I don't think—"

"You have no clue, Sara," the man said. "Now shut—"

"Edward Mullin," a loud voice boomed. "You

will be awarded five million dollars for killing the monster!" Heavy applause filled the area, hurting Lon's ears. Once the applause died down, the voice said, "Tag the dog and we will fill the provided bank account with your winnings."

"Told you it's five million," the woman said.

"Oh, shut it," one of the men said and added. "Go ahead and tag it, Eddie."

"Don't call me Eddie, Carl. You know better."

A few chuckles rustled through the mob.

Lon remained still, heart thudding. Saliva filled his mouth, and he swallowed it down quickly. Someone was approaching. The man's scent was tinged with engine oil and onions. An older man from what Lon could glean from his scent. The blood pumped sluggishly, like molasses through a dime-sized tubes. The man's arteries were hardening and would be dead in a year. Maybe less.

"Ya got the tag, Ed?"

"What the hell do you think I got in my hand, Carl?"

More chuckles littered the mob.

Ed was only about five feet away. The old man took another step and Lon sprang onto all fours. Ed sucked in a sharp breath and stopped. His eyes were wide, mouth gaping.

"Oh shit," someone said.

Lon pounced onto Ed, driving him to the ground and immediately buried his teeth into the old man's throat. He sucked down a mouthful of blood, ripped a large chunk of flesh out and swallowed. He tore into the man's stomach. The easiest, quickest meal. He feasted on various organs. He rammed a claw up into the ribcage and scooped out one of Ed's lungs.

"Oh my god," someone said, sounding sick. Lon was too busy feeding to care who it was.

Ed's heart tasted foul, and he tossed it aside. The man ate a lot of bad foods. Greasy foods, by the overly salty taste.

He was munching on the other lung when someone shot him. It was like getting pricked with a small needle. Lon glared at the mob in front of him, still gnawing on the lung. A few men raised their rifles and shotguns.

Lon grinned. Blood mixed with saliva trickled through the fur on his chin.

"Fire," a large man shouted.

Lon leaped off Ed and crashed into the mob. Men and women alike shrieked as he slashed through them. He took hefty bites out of each one, gaining more and more strength.

He shoved a woman aside and smacked a shotgun out of the hands of a short man wearing a stained red hat. He slashed the short man's throat with one claw and cut deep grooves across the face with the other. The man screamed through the bloody hole in his face that used to be a mouth. Lon jumped onto his shoulders and launched at another man. This one much taller with a considerable belly. Lon slammed him to ground and tore into his chest. He crushed the ribcage, snapped ribs like pretzels, and clawed out the man's still beating heart. Lon ate as much as he could before a buckshot slammed into him and shoved him off the man.

He rolled and rose on his hind legs, looming over

the man with the shotgun. The buckshot wound was already healed.

The mob scattered, leaving the man with the shotgun alone. They jumped into trucks and other vehicles and squealed away.

Lon snorted and focused on the lone man.

The man gaped up at Lon. The shotgun tumbled from his trembling hands. He backed away, tripped over the tall man's corpse, and fell hard on his ass.

"P… Please," the man blubbered. "I… I'm sorry. I… I…"

Lon lunged and twisted the man's chubby head off his chubby body. The body flopped onto the tall man's corpse. Somewhere nearby, an owl hooted. Lon tossed the head aside and glanced around at all the carnage. He huffed a breath through his nostrils.

Now we run, the human part said. *Get as far away from this town as we can.*

Lon grunted. The game was over, but the human part was right. He needed to get away from the town. He needed to be free. He…

Soft buzzing piqued his attention. He caught a glimpse of one of the drones flying away from town.

Let it go, the human part said. *We need to leave.*

But Lon shook his vulpine head and began following the drone.

CHAPTER 29

THE DRONE FLEW for miles.

Lon felt the itch of dawn approaching.

Then the drone veered into dense woods. Lon followed until the drone dipped through the canopy and to a hallow. Lon crept close enough to watch the ground open up and the drone slip through the opening.

He sprang forward as the ground began to close and slid through a millisecond before it closed.

Darkness literally swallowed him as he slid down a large metal tube. Eventually, he fell into a shallow pool of water. A cave? He stood and glanced around, searching for the drone. Slight buzzing snagged his attention to the left. He caught a slim glimpse of the drone slipping into a tunnel.

Moving as quietly as he could, Lon followed the drone to a dimly lit room with moldy walls. A door slid up into the ceiling, giving way to a narrow opening. White light spilled through, catching Lon in its glare. He scrambled back into the shadows.

The drone flew through the bright opening and Lon followed, narrowly avoiding the door, which slammed down like a guillotine. He shuddered, knowing how close he came to being sliced vertically in half, and followed the drone down a corridor of polished metal. His reflection stretched along the walls and ceiling like warm taffy. He tried to ignore it and focus on the little black drone buzzing along on its merry path.

The drone was spherical, except for the bottom where the propeller was, or whatever moved the thing along. A little different from the others Lon saw around town. The drones in town were more like frisbees with the middles punched out and a few propellers on top.

Lon followed the spherical drone down the mirrored hall. It made a sluggish buzzing sound, like a fat black fly on a hot, lazy day in August having gorged itself on offal. A low, slow bumbling sound.

At any moment he could be spotted. If the drone turned around and saw him…

He crept forward, keeping most of his attention on the drone. If it turned, he would bash it against the walls. From there, he didn't know what he'd do other than keep moving forward.

But the drone didn't turn around. It didn't even slow down. Just continued buzzing onward down the mirrored hallway.

Eventually, the hall came to an end at another door, which slid up into the ceiling like the last one.

The drone wasted no time and darted through the doorway. Lon sprinted through the doorway, once more almost getting sliced in half from top to bottom.

A beep snagged his attention. The drone whirred, turned around, and backed into an inverted charging station next to other spherical drones.

Lon froze, staring at the drone as a small red light near the top winked out.

He waited for what felt like hours, but nothing happened. No one came for him. Gradually, he relaxed. A small shot of piss squirted onto the floor. Lon shivered and walked around the small room. He passed by it a couple times... then saw it.

Optical illusion, the human part said.

Lon, the dog part, didn't really understand what that meant, but there sure as hell was the open doorway hiding just around the curve of the charging shelf that held the drones. He hadn't noticed it at first.

He slinked through the doorway and into another hallway. This one was very short, though and barely lit by a single raw bulb dangling on a couple wires from the paneled ceiling. It was as if he stepped back in time to the human part's grandma's house. A memory that hadn't surfaced in more than a decade. Lon shivered from intensity of it. Even though it was before his part merged with the human part. Before they became one. He felt the human part's deep nostalgia and longing. Something Lon couldn't fully understand.

At the end of the hallway was a closed door. A

normal one with a knob.

Lon's eyes shifted back and forth, searching for a trap. If there was one, he couldn't see, nor smell it. But there was a sound. Clapping? Shouting? A crowd of people making noise.

Lon moved to the door, gripped the knob in his long claw, and turned it. He pulled the open. The hinges creaked slightly. The room beyond the door stopped him. Black cords snaked along a concrete floor. Everything was covered in black cloth. The noise of a crowd was ten times louder. He crept into the room, which gave off to a pathway. The pathway opened to…

People darted back and forth. A tall man wearing a suit and shiny black hair, shouted at a woman to get her shit together and find Randy.

"Y'all ready for a dog fight?" A familiar voice boomed.

The crowd erupted into screaming and howling so loud it hurt Lon's ears. He whined from it and backed away a few feet. The noise was so loud, he didn't notice a woman screaming after spotting him. He didn't notice the people running away and men with guns approaching the mouth of the pathway.

The noise. It drove silvery spikes into his brain. He fought in small arenas with large crowds and noise was like that. Loud and shrill. Something that nearly drove him insane every night as it was now.

Lon shook his head and tried to focus.

He managed a few steps forward as the men with guns charged in. The crowd's screaming swelled.

There was nothing he could do. The men with guns, the swelling noise… the spikes digging into his brain…

Lon roared, sprang forward and slashed one of the men across the face with his right claw, sheering most of his face off. The man wailed and fired his gun wildly. A bullet struck one of the other men in the chest. Another bullet blew a hole in the back of a woman's head. Lon bit the man's throat out, chomped down the flesh and leaped onto another of the armed men. He ripped into the abdomen as the man screamed, yanking out a liver and eating as much of it as he could.

Energy pulsed through him. Strength. The more he ate the better he felt. Unstoppable.

From the man with the open abdomen, Lon slammed into yet another armed man. The others, radioing someone, ran away. The entire room cleared as Lon tore the man's lower jaw off and tossed it aside. The man yowled, pink tongue flailing in gore. Lon clawed one of the man's meaty arms off at the shoulder and walked away, eating the arm like a chicken leg.

There was a reason he was here. In the belly of the beast.

CHAPTER 30

"SORRY, FOLKS," RODNEY said and waved at the audience. He beamed a smile at them for good measure. "I'm getting word through my earpiece to end the show and send y'all home."

The audience booed and Rodney nodded. He held up his arms, feigning surrender. "Hey, now, don't shoot the messenger."

In all honesty, though, Rodney had had enough for the night. The dog was loose somewhere in the studio, and he was just fucking over it. Too tired to care. He wanted to tell them all to fuck off right now, but that would put a stain on his career he couldn't afford. He had seven children to feed, after all. None of them lived with him, thank god, but the courts forced him to pay their slutty mothers. If it was up to him, they wouldn't get a goddamn cent. Maybe they should have gotten abortions when they were still legal.

He smiled at the audience. "Out y'all go now. Tomorrow nigh—"

The audience erupted into screams. Not fun screams, but something else. Rodney frowned and lowered the mic. The people were trying to leave, but not in a way that was at all orderly. They crawled over each other, trampled each other, shoved and bit each other. Shrieks of pain mingled with screams of terror. Desperate, wild cries for help.

Rodney stood on the stage, arms dangling at his sides, gaping at all the people literally killing each other to get to the doors. Speaking of doors, they were clogged with people. People pushing. People punching and kicking. People clawing at one another. Screaming and shrieking and wailing. He watched a woman jam a thumb deep into a man's eye, all the way to the second knuckle. Two men picked an elderly woman up and flung her at the human barricade at the doors.

And that's what it was. A human barricade. Dead people, injured people, people shoving and screaming and clawing at each other…

The entire scene was madness. Sheer and utter madness. He'd never seen anything like it. And he had seen some wild shit over the years.

Then, very close, a guttural growl.

Rodney sucked in a sharp breath and his bladder released a hot stream of piss down his leg, soaking his tailored slacks. High thread count. Very expensive. Ruined.

The screams of the audience fell to the wayside.

Hot, rancid breaths puffed against Rodney's sweaty cheek.

"L-Listen," Rodney managed, heart crashing into his ribs. "I-If you want the bosses, I can—"

The dog slammed Rodney onto the stage floor. He tried to scramble to his feet, but the dog slammed him down again, much harder. Something in his right arm snapped and he cried out in agony. Before he could try to crawl away, the dog rolled him over onto his back and roared into his face.

Rodney screamed then. He screamed so loud one his vocal cords ruptured turning his scream into a hollow whistle.

The dog grinned, revealing a lot of sharp teeth. A runner of hot drool seeped onto Rodney's cheek. A whine slipped from his throat and leaked out of his quivering mouth. A deep growl trembled the sliver of air between him and the dog.

"P-Please," Rodney said. "D-Don't do this." Tears trickled down the sides of his face. "Th-They hired me to do this. It... It's nothing personal."

The dog grunted and looked at the audience literally killing each other to get away from him. Rodney took the moment to pull his pistol from under his suit jacket and—

The dog shifted to the side and clutched Rodney's arm in its jaws. The pain of those sharp teeth sinking into his skin, muscle, all the way to the bone, was so intense his bowels released with a loud *blurrrt*. The pistol thumped to the stage floor. The dog shook its head and tore a large chunk of Rodney's arm off. He screamed from pain and terror and tried crawling away from the dog, but the monster dragged him back, claws puncturing his thighs.

Rodney shrieked, struggled like a worm because the use of his arms were so limited.

The dog flipped him over onto his back and the last thing Rodney saw were those sharp teeth lunging at his face.

CHAPTER 31

LON ATE THE stage man's throat out and reared.

The people were still panicking. There was a small part of him that craved their flesh, but on the other hand, he was full. If he ate too much, he might get sluggish and he couldn't have that.

Lon turned away from the shrieking crowd and dashed backstage. He didn't know who he was looking for, but he knew the type. He saw them all the time at the fights. The men in suits. The men in charge. Yes, he knew the type well...

Backstage was barren. Anyone who had lingered after he revealed his presence was now long gone. He took to the white hallways, taking in every scent. Nothing stuck out. Nothing familiar either. Still, he wandered the halls, peeking into rooms as he went.

He was about to give up and try a different part of the building when a slight whiff of cologne stopped him near a closed door. Lon's muzzle wrinkled into a snarl. Yes. He knew the scent. He remembered it. He hated it. Images associated to the man's cologne shuffled through his mind. A steel rod prodded at him while being locked in his cage. Mean laughter. The man with his pursed lips and fake looking brown hair with a strange fluffy, yet thin semi-pompadour that was obviously a way to hide the balding. Which was also obvious he had a scalp reduction. At least that's what the human part told him at the time, anyway. Lon, the dog, had no idea what that meant. He had an idea, but…

Lon followed the noxious scent closer to the closed door. He sniffed and grimaced. Yes. It was him in there. He held in a growl and backed away from the door.

DOUG TREMP

HE HAD NO idea where everyone went and didn't care.

Doug brought out a bottle of Adderall. Prescription, of course. Can't have people thinking he was doing some kind of drug. He shook out three pills and smiled. He'd been waiting all fucking day for this. Just a little… something. Something that would get him through the crowds of people and to his limo. Something that helped him appear jovial, which was like his goddamn trademark. Happy Doug, they all called him. It's true…

The door was locked and the dog was inside the building, but that didn't matter. It wasn't like a dog, even the one on the show, knew who he was and would seek him out.

Doug chuckled to himself and used one of his credit cards to crush up the pills into a fine powder.

He rolled a hundred-dollar bill into a small tube. Cliché, sure, but it worked fucking great. Doug snorted the line of powder, coughed and leaned back in the chair, rubbing his nose. He sniffed and giggled, already beginning to feel what he called, "the lift". The magic of it never ceased to amaze him.

After another minute or so, he wiped the residue off the table and hopped out of his chair. He paced the room a bit, heart thrumming, brain in hyperdrive. He checked his phone a dozen time within a minute. He drew a penis on the dry erase board, chuckled, and erased it with a giggle.

Okay, this was better. Now he could appear younger and energetic to the paparazzi if they were hovering around and maybe they wouldn't associate him to much with the Dog Foundation. He was just checking out what was going on in a building he owned, that's all. No one would be the wiser. Social media tabloids be damned.

Doug sighed, gliding on the high, straightened his suit jacket and walked toward the door. Maybe he could—

The door slammed open, and a monstrous figure stepped into the room. It towered over Doug. The top of its head touched the ceiling. Its ears curled at the tips. Its yellow eyes fixed on him. A deep growl shook the air between them. Its muzzle wrinkled, revealing long, sharp teeth.

Doug, heart literally thrumming at rapid pace, quickened even more. His bladder let go, spilling hot piss down his right leg.

The dog sniffed, grunted and leaned forward

until its muzzle was mere inches from Doug's sweaty face. Again, its growl literally shook the air between them. Or he was so high it felt like it, but…

Doug giggled and held his arms up a bit. "Okay, okay." He smiled. "You found me. Hey, let's try something. You want to try something? Look…" He backed away another couple feet and held up a phone. "I can call the other guys. Have them meet me here." Doug grinned. "Would you like that?"

CHAPTER 32

LON FROWNED. What was the man up to?

"Yeah, you'd like that. More bang for your buck, right? Huge. Look, I will… these guys are really bad people. Not me. Not me. I don't make any of the rules."

Lon grunted.

Doug chuckled, wiped sweat from his forehead and tapped his phone. Through the speakerphone, another man said, "The hell you want? We're going into hiding. I thought—"

"Hey, Jeff," Doug said and gave Lon a thumbs up. "I'm trapped here. Can you come get me?"

"Doug, I—"

"How's that nice free condo up in Manhattan treating your mistress, Jeff?"

A brief pause followed.

"We'll swing back around and come get you,"

Jeff said. "Can you meet us outside?"

Doug dropped Lon a wink. "I'm trapped in the media room right now. They're animals. Animals."

Another brief pause.

"Okay, Micheal and I will come in and get ya."

"I found something while you were away, though," Doug said and smiled at Lon. "I think Randy missed a loophole in the contracts. It's huge."

"So, bring it along, then," Jeff said. "We don't have time to—"

"I can't," Doug said and glanced at Lon. The man was sweating heavily now. It trickled down his orange, fake tanned face. Lon recoiled a bit at the stench of it.

Something was wrong with the man. Some kind of illness. It was in his sweat. In the spittle that flew from his pursed lips as he spoke.

Doug was sick. Not just mentally either.

"I need you all to get the fuck over here," Doug said, voice getting louder. "This involves all of us and it's time sensitive."

Jeff didn't say anything for a minute or two.

Lon moved closer to Doug. Enough was enou—

"Sit tight, then," Jeff said. "We'll be there in a few minutes."

Doug sighed and smiled. He shot Lon a thumbs up. "Good. I'll get it ready so we can get it over with."

"You do that," Jeff said. "See ya soon."

Doug hung up and beamed a smile at Lon. "There. They're all going to be here in a few. I'm great at negotiations, but you know that. Look...

you saw it. Okay? You saw it. I'm great at negotiations." He waved a hand and chuckled. "Now I want to make a deal."

Lon blinked.

"You let me go right now and you get all the other guys responsible for everything." Doug nodded and pointed at the door. "They'll be coming through there any minute now." He straightened and smiled at Lon. "We got a deal, then? I got you the other guys, so you can let me go. The deal. I'm fantastic at making deals. It's true. Look… I own a lot of buildings in New York. A lot. I could—"

Lon tore off most of the man's ugly face. One of his nails snagged an eye socket, splitting the eyeball. Doug shrieked and whirled away. His small hands slapped onto the remnants of skin still on his face. Limp shreds barely clinging to his scalp. Still shrieking, split eyeball oozing down his bloody face, Doug searched the floor for the rest of his face while trying to piece together what remained attached to him.

"Oh… my god…"

Lon turned and faced the men responsible for the dog fights. Responsible for his enslavement. The men who controlled everything and tried to kill him and make a profit doing it.

A deep growl quaked in his throat and chest. The men, four in all, backed away from the doorway. Behind him, Doug continued shrieking.

One of the men, the taller bald one, drew a pistol from its shoulder holster under his dark blue suit jacket and pointed it at Lon.

"Holy shit," one of the other men said. "I didn't

know you carried a gun."

"Now's not the time, Mike," the bald man said, his focus fixed on Lon. "Get out of here."

"And leave you alone?" Another man said. This one shorter than the other two with black hair swept off to one side. "I don't think—"

"I'm the only one with a gun," the bald man snapped. "Now get the hell outta—"

Lon rushed forward, grabbed the bald man's gun arm and snapped it at the elbow. The pistol dropped to the floor and the bald man staggered backward, gaping at his ruined arm.

"Oh, fu—" Mike managed before Lon barreled into the small group of men.

He tore through each of them like fat bags of blood.

Once it was over, he slumped in mild exhaustion and ate a couple of hearts.

Meanwhile, Doug was still wailing. Still trying to piece his face back together over the bloody mess where it used to be.

Lon almost left him like that. Almost. He loomed over Doug and the man's remaining eyeball rolled up to gape at him.

Doug screamed and thrashed away until his back slammed against the wall near the white board.

Lon bashed Doug's head against the wall hard enough to break through the drywall. Nothing to really hurt the man, but enough to shock the bastard into stunned silence for a few seconds or so. Before Doug could scream again, Lon plunged his right claw into the man's chest. He broke through the ribs and felt the man's lungs.

Doug's entire body quaked. He uttered a weak, breathless whine.

Lon grinned, sank his claw into the man's lung and ripped it out.

Doug's lipless mouth gapped, white teeth stained with blood, as he tried to breathe. His hands gripped the fur of Lon's chest, pulling out handfuls as he sank to the floor. Lon watched the man drown in his own blood, which took longer than it should have. The bastard had too much fight in him. Evil was hard to kill, after all.

Lon slumped. Weariness stole over him, and he staggered out of the room. He stepped over the mutilated corpses, found an exit door and stepped outside into the night.

CHAPTER 33

HE WOKE THE next morning in the loft of some old barn somewhere in the middle of nowhere.

The human part of Lon groaned and rolled out from under a blanket of hay. He sneezed from all the dust and sat up. He picked hay stems out of his hair and blinked. Birds flitted from the wooden beams. Sunlight filtered through the grimy, opaque windows, highlighting floating motes of dust.

He leaned over to look down onto the main floor of the barn. It stood empty. All the metal appeared rusted. The floor was covered in years of bird shit, bat shit and dirt. Lon moved and the boards under him creaked. The birds scattered for a few seconds then returned to their perches.

Naked, he climbed out of the loft and ventured out of the barn. He stood in thigh-high weeds as grasshoppers flicked away in every direction. He was on a island in an emerald sea. A warm breeze lifted the hair away from his face. Sweaty and covered in hay dust. In every direction was a sea of corn. He squinted from the bright, hot sun baking into his bare skin.

Summer winds whispered through the corn and rustled the tall grass around him and the barn. And except for the birds singing in the barn behind him, the world was... quiet. No one was shouting or cheering or booing. No one was doing anything. Not a whimper.

Lon sighed, a smiling playing at his chapped lips, and walked into the sea of corn.

The leaves scratched him as he ventured deeper and deeper, but he barely noticed. He walked faster. Then jogged. Before he knew it, he sprinted through the corn. The corn leaves sliced his skin like razors. Blood mixed with sweat smeared his skin. Didn't matter.

A tang in the air drove him onward, ignoring the tiny slices of pain and the blood. Ignoring everything except that singular scent enhanced by the dog part of him. A deep mineral aroma. Nothing bad or wrong. Nothing curious, but familiar. Something his entire body yearned for.

The corn abruptly ended. Lon slid down a small slope choked with weeds, brambles and saplings until he slipped on muddy bank. He landed on his side, groaned and rolled on his back. He gaped at the blue sky and burst into laughter. Loud, raucous laughter. He laughed until his throat burned from the strain and turned his head to the side. A smile lengthened on his grimy face at the small creek no more than four feet away from him.

Lon, chuckling, rolled into the swift, cold water of the creek. Which was more like a trout stream. Clear and constantly moving.

And it was cold as hell.

He sank to the bottom, bare back smashing against the rocky and sandy stream floor, then floated to the surface. All the blood and grime and dirt and death, clouded around him before being swept downstream.

Lon spread his arms out and floated in the cool water for a moment before the current stole him away.

The stream carried him for miles and the entire time he couldn't stop smiling.

Only one word echoed through his head.

Finally.

Finally… he was free.

ABOUT THE AUTHOR

LUCAS PEDERSON is an American novelist and short story writer of horror, dark fantasy, young adult and science fiction. He lives in a small Iowa town with his family and they're all pretty sure their cat is an alien. He can be reached at lucaspederson@yahoo.com, Twitter, Instagram, and Facebook.